Wilbur and Orville Wright

Young Fliers

Illustrated by Robert Doremus

Wilbur and Orville Wright

Young Fliers

By Augusta Stevenson

Aladdin Paperbacks

Aladdin Paperbacks
An imprint of Simon & Schuster
Children's Publishing Division
1230 Avenue of the Americas
New York, NY 10020
Copyright © 1951, 1959 by the Bobbs-Merrill Company, Inc.
All rights reserved including the right of reproduction
in whole or in part in any form.

First Aladdin Paperbacks edition, 1986
Printed in the United States of America

30 29 28 27 26 25 24

Library of Congress Cataloging-in-Publication Data

Stevenson, Augusta.
    Wilbur and Orville Wright, young fliers.

    Reprint. Previously published: Wilbur and
Orville Wright, boys with wings. Indianapolis :
Bobbs Merrill Co., 1984. (Childhood of famous Americans)
    Summary: Presents the boyhood of the brothers who
flew the first airplane in 1903.
    1. Wright, Wilbur, 1867–1912—Juvenile literature.
2. Wright, Orville, 1871–1948—Juvenile literature.
3. Aeronautics—United States—Biography—Juvenile
literature. [1. Wright Wilbur, 1867–1912. 2. Wright,
Orville, 1871–1948. 3. Aeronautics—Biography]
I. Title. II. Series: Childhood of famous Americans.
[TL540.W7S73 1996]   629.13'0092'2 [B] [920] 86-10747
ISBN 0-02-042170-2

To my brother,
Mr. Benjamin Stevenson

Illustrations

Full pages

Numerous smaller illustrations

Contents

CHILDHOOD OF FAMOUS AMERICANS

Books by Augusta Stevenson

⋆ ⋆ Wilbur and Orville Wright

Young Fliers

Both Boys Took
after Grandpa

Most of the houses on Hawthorne Street in Dayton, Ohio, were close together with narrow yards between. The Wright house was so close to its neighbors that the people next door always knew when the four Wright boys were noisy.

Mrs. Pruitt, on the right, said they were noisy all the time unless they were in school. They were either playing in the yard and yelling like wild Indians or hammering in their woodshed.

Mrs. Thomas, on the left, said she didn't mind their hammering. She thought it was wonderful that the Wright boys liked to make things.

"Why," she went on, "the two oldest boys are

11

making a big cart now. And Reuchlin is only sixteen. And Lorin is only fourteen. But they aren't making very much noise."

"Yes, but that nine-year-old Wilbur has been making up for it. For the last week he has been making wooden whistles and blowing them."

"I know. His mother told me. She said he whittled them out by himself."

"He had plenty of help blowing them. They were all at it. That youngest boy, Orville, even gave his sister a whistle."

"She couldn't blow it. Katie is only two years old."

"She tried. She wouldn't be a Wright if she didn't try to do things."

"Well, they are certainly trying to do something this morning. They've been shouting and laughing for the last half hour."

"They woke me up. I never heard them make such a racket so early."

Even the Sines family heard them, and they lived in the second house from the Wrights on Hawthorne.

"Those boys must think it's the Fourth of July," said Mr. Sines. "All they need is a bunch of firecrackers."

This made Mrs. Sines think of the date. "Isn't this August nineteenth?" she asked.

"It is, and it's 1876 too, in case you've forgotten."

"Then it's Orville Wright's birthday. He is five years old today."

"I'm five years old too," said Eddie Sines.

"You are just one month older than Orville. That's why I remember."

"What are they laughing at?"

"Maybe Orville got a funny present," said his father.

He was right. Orville had received a funny present. It was only a small top, but it was the strangest-looking top the Wright boys had ever seen. There wasn't one like it in the Dayton stores.

Their father had bought it in Cincinnati, Ohio. It was the first top of this kind he had ever seen himself. And he had traveled a good deal. He was a preacher, and church affairs took him to many different places.

"I wanted you boys to have this top," he said. "The clerk said it was a scientific top. He called it a gyroscope."

Roosh (short for Reuchlin) understood this. Lorin had a sort of idea what it meant. But Wilbur didn't know, and of course young Orville didn't.

The two younger boys just knew the new top wasn't pretty and shiny like their old one. It didn't have any red and green stripes, either. But it had to be wound up with a string and it would spin.

There wasn't much to it. There was only a round piece of lead a little larger than a silver dollar. It was also a little thicker. A metal spindle went through the center. And around the lead and the spindle were two heavy metal bands.

In the upper part of the spindle was a small slit for threading the string. In the end of the lower part was a tiny groove. Wilbur was the first to discover this and to ask why it was there.

"It's a sort of foot to clutch some small object," his father explained. "It holds the top there while it is spinning."

"What kind of object?"

"The clerk said it would spin on the point of a pencil. Let's try it. Hold this pencil steady, Lorin, with the point up. Wind the top, Roosh, and when it spins put it on the pencil point."

The boys obeyed. Then everyone began to laugh. The top was spinning on the point.

16

"It acts as if it were alive," said Wilbur.

"And just as if it knew it wouldn't fall," said his mother.

"That's where science comes in," said Mr. Wright. "It will keep its balance till it runs down. No matter which way I tilt it, the top will stay in that position as long as the wheel is spinning fast."

"Someday they may use gyroscopes on steamships," declared Roosh. "My teacher said so. He said they may help to balance ships, no matter how high the waves are."

Now Wilbur and Orville asked questions. Would ships have big tops? How big would they be? Would they spin about all over the decks?

"They wouldn't be tops, boys, but big machines that act by the same law of science. And they'd keep ships from rolling."

Wilbur and Orville were still curious. They thought of more questions, but now it was seven o'clock. Breakfast was ready, and the top had to be laid aside for a while.

BUT WILBUR AND ORVILLE HAD IDEAS TOO

Mr. Wright had been telling them about the string-walk. He said the clerk had told him the top could walk across a string, just like a tight-rope walker at a circus.

The boys were ready to try this. Wilbur and Lorin were about the same height so they held the short piece of twine. They held it tightly to keep it from sagging.

Then Roosh spun the top and put it on the string at Wilbur's end. An amazing thing happened. The top walked along the string to Lorin's end. And it was spinning all the time.

"It *is* like a tightrope walker," declared Mrs. Wright. "See how it tips from side to side to keep its balance!"

If the neighbors were listening now they would certainly hear more shouting and laughter. Even little Katie was laughing and clapping her hands.

The two younger boys wanted to do the "walk" again, but their brothers had to go. It was Saturday and they had half-day work in a grocery.

A little later Mrs. Wright saw Orville and Wilbur go to the woodshed. She thought nothing of it—they often played out there. It was too bad she didn't see them when they came back for the hatchet and screwdriver.

Roosh and Lorin hurried home at noon. There were several things they wanted to try with the top. As they came through the front gate they saw their mother on the porch.

"I've been waiting for you," she said softly when they joined her. "I want to tell you something before you go in. The top is broken."

"Broken!"

"Your brothers wanted to see if it would spin without the metal bands."

"So they took them off!" cried Roosh. "Was the lead broken?"

"It was cracked. They feel very sad about it. They have both been crying."

"They ought to cry," said Lorin.

"Wasn't Father angry with them?" asked Roosh.

"No, and I wasn't either. They aren't to

blame, boys. It was born in them to see how things were made. My father did it all his life and they are exactly like him."

"But I thought Grandpa put things together," said Roosh. "Father said he made the best wagons and carriages in the state."

"That's true, but do you know how it happened? He took old wagons and carriages apart. He studied them and then he made his better."

"I believe Orvy is like him," said Lorin. "Orvy took his toy duck apart to see what made it quack."

"Wilbur must be like him too," said Roosh. "He is always taking old clocks apart. I won't scold them about breaking the top."

"Neither will I," said Lorin. "Mother, do you think they will make wagons and carriages when they grow up?"

"I don't know about that. But I'm sure they'll

make something if we don't fuss too much when they take things apart. Come now, let's go in. And, remember, don't scold the boys."

THE MYSTERIOUS SEWING MACHINE

Orville Wright and Edward Sines were to enter kindergarten one morning. It had all been arranged. The teacher was expecting them and Mrs. Sines was to take them. Orville was waiting for her and Eddie.

But Eddie came alone. He said his mother couldn't go to the school. And could he go with Orvy and someone?

Mrs. Wright said Roosh or Lorin would take them. But Roosh said he was late now for his first class. He would have to run all the way. Lorin said he was late too, and he had to run.

So it was Wilbur who started out with them. He didn't mind; they wouldn't be any trouble.

And they weren't, for about three minutes. After that they were nothing but trouble.

They ran through puddles and splashed muddy water on their clean clothes. Wet and muddy shoes didn't seem to bother them. They rubbed their hands on old fences and gates. They picked up dirty papers.

Finally Wilbur had to lead them. He held their hands so tightly they couldn't get away. A dozen times he wished Mrs. Sines had brought them. At last he asked Eddie why she didn't.

"She had to wait for her new sewing machine. A man was coming with it."

Wilbur was interested. "What did she do with her old machine?"

"Pa put it in the barn. He said I could play with it."

Now Orville was interested. "Can I play with it, too?"

"Yes, so can Wilbur. Ma said you could."

"I'd like to see if it's like ours," said Wilbur. "I can take that apart and oil it. I can put it together again too."

"You can't," said Eddie.

"He can," said Orville. "I've watched him."

"Come on," said Wilbur. "I'll show you."

An hour later the school janitor called on the two families. He said their boys hadn't come to kindergarten this morning. The teacher would like to know why.

The parents were astonished. They had sent the children. What had happened? Perhaps Wilbur hadn't gone all the way with them. Perhaps they had turned at the corner where Wilbur left them instead of going straight on.

If they had, they would be going to the river. They might be there now—there had been time enough. The very thought frightened the parents. It would be easy for the boys to slip on wet rocks and fall into the water.

It had taken only an instant to think of all this. The next instant the two fathers were running to the Sineses' barn. They would drive to the river in Mr. Sines's buggy. The children would hardly be able to walk back. It was too far.

"The men ought to drive to the school first and talk with Wilbur," said Mrs. Wright. "He might know where the boys are. Let's run after them and tell them."

They followed the men so quickly that they went into the barn just behind them. So all four saw the strange sight at the same time. There, over in a corner, were the lost children! And Wilbur was with them!

They were working on the old sewing machine. It had been taken apart. Pieces were all about them on the floor. Wilbur was showing Orville how to get the pedals off. Eddie was watching.

They were so interested that they hadn't heard their parents enter. When Mr. Wright spoke they jumped. Then Wilbur hurried to explain: "We haven't been here very long. We just thought we'd play a little while. Why, it isn't late, is it?"

"It's ten o'clock," replied his mother. "We were looking for you."

"Ten o'clock!" cried the astonished boy.

"Don't stop to talk," said his mother. "Hurry to school."

"I ought to put the machine together first."

"You can do that any time," said Mrs. Sines.

"Why couldn't I do it now, Mother? It's too late to go this morning. The teacher doesn't like us to be late."

"Pick up your books and go straight to school," said his father sternly. "We will take the boys to kindergarten."

"I don't know what to tell the teacher."

"Tell her the truth."

"Yes, sir." Then Wilbur went running.

"I don't want to go to kindergarten," said Orville. "I want to play with the machine. It's more fun."

"I don't want to go either," said Eddie.

But they went. Both mothers took them.

That evening Mr. and Mrs. Sines were talking things over. Mrs. Sines said she had watched Wilbur put the machine together that afternoon.

"I never saw anything like it," she declared. "Why, even little Orvy knew just what to do. He would hand the right parts to his brother every time."

"Well, their Grandfather Koerner is wonderful with tools. He could probably make a sewing machine blindfolded. And he would probably love every piece of it."

"That's the way the boys acted—as if they loved to handle the parts."

"Well, I guess we'd better begin to save our money."

"For what?"

"For a carriage made by Mr. Wilbur and Mr. Orville Wright."

"I wouldn't be surprised if they made one."

"I would be surprised if they didn't."

The Velvet Collar and Cuffs

ANOTHER member of the Wright family took after Grandfather Koerner. This was their mother, Mrs. Susan Koerner Wright. She loved to make things. Her father had taught her how to use tools when she was a girl.

Only this week she had mended a broken chair, a picture frame, the coffee grinder and the china head of Katie's doll.

She had made several things for the house last year. The nice shelves in the kitchen, a footstool and a stand. She had also made a sled for the boys. They all said it looked exactly like the store sleds.

Susan Wright was also a fine seamstress. She made her own clothes and Katie's. She made over the boys' suits if they were still good enough. They were passed on right down the line. Mr. Wright's old suits were used for Roosh. Roosh's went to Lorin. Lorin's to Wilbur. Wilbur's to Orville.

The suits were so well made the boys were proud of them. They couldn't see any difference between their clothes and those of their schoolmates. They were glad that their mother was so clever.

It was a good thing Susan knew how to save. The Reverend Milton Wright didn't get a large salary. His church was small and he couldn't afford to pay much. So Mrs. Wright didn't buy one thing they could do without.

With all this saving and making-over they were able to put away a little money every month. Mr. Wright told the boys it was for a rainy day. "There might come a time when I can't work," he said. "Then we will have something to live on."

At once Wilbur began to save for his rainy day. He picked up old nails, screws, bolts, hinges and rusty keys from streets and alleys. He said he might need them by and by. He wanted to make several things as soon as he had time.

Just now he was too busy. He was trying to learn a piece to speak at school. There would be a program on the last day of the fall term. This was only one week away.

Mrs. Wright thought the piece was too long for a boy of ten and a half. It had eight verses and each verse had six lines. Wilbur was sure he could learn them if the family didn't bother him.

Everyone left him alone. Mrs. Wright didn't even tell him about the suit she was making over for him. She told the rest of the family she had

had to wait for some goods. The suit probably wouldn't be finished till the last minute.

The last night came and she was still working. But she said he would find it in his room the next morning. And sure enough, there it was on the chair by his bed when he woke up.

He got up quickly and looked at it. Then his heart sank. He wouldn't wear it! Why had his mother made this awful-looking coat? Why had she made the collar and cuffs of *velvet?*

Only girls wore velvet. He had never seen a boy in a velvet-trimmed coat. Wouldn't the other boys make fun of him if he wore this! He could see them now winking at one another.

He couldn't speak his piece with them grinning at him. He'd forget it. He'd rather wear his old suit even if the knees were patched. Maybe he would. He could hide this new one and slide down the rain pipe.

Anyway, he'd have to wear it down to break-

fast. His mother had told him to put it on this
morning. And he wouldn't say a word about
the velvet. He didn't want to hurt her feelings.

34

Then he dressed. But before he went down-stairs he took a good look at the rain pipe.

DID HE HAVE THE COURAGE TO FACE THEM?

"Your suit looks fine!" exclaimed Mrs. Wright. "It fits you, too."

"What's that on the collar?" asked Orville. "It's on the cuffs, too."

"It's velvet. Boys' coats are being trimmed with that now, Wilbur. I saw several in my latest fashion magazine."

Wilbur didn't say anything. He was eating and he pretended to be in a hurry.

Mrs. Wright went on. "I am so glad I had the suit ready for you to wear today."

"She sewed all night," said Orville. "I heard Father tell Roosh."

"Mother! You shouldn't have done that. I could have worn my old suit."

35

"With the patched knees! Indeed you couldn't! Your classmates will all wear their best clothes. And there will be visitors. I'm going myself."

Wilbur nearly choked on his oatmeal. But he managed to say he was glad.

"Your father is going too, if he can. He was delighted with the way I made your suit. He didn't think I could do it. It was Lorin's, you know. The collar and cuffs were worn out and I couldn't find any cloth to match. This velvet settled everything."

It certainly did, thought Wilbur as he went up to his room. It was almost time to go. He would have to decide what to do.

Then Orville came. There was only afternoon school for the first grade. So he was always asking Wilbur what he could do in the mornings. Just now he wanted to know what to do about the cart for Katie's doll.

36

He said he had a box but he didn't know how to make wheels.

"Make them out of cardboard. I'll help you make wooden wheels tomorrow. Now go away, Orvy. I have to get ready."

"You are ready."

"I want to say my piece again."

Orville left then and Wilbur closed the door. But he didn't say his piece. He just sat on his bed and tried to think of some plan. Maybe he'd stay at home today. He could say he didn't feel like going to school. And that would be the truth; he didn't.

Then he thought about his mother's working all night on his suit. He remembered how happy she had looked when she saw how well it fitted him. And he knew how pleased she was with the velvet.

He jumped to his feet. He knew now what he would do. He wouldn't disappoint her. The boys could laugh all they wanted to. So could the girls. He'd pay no attention. He'd face them! He'd even act proud of his new suit!

Wilbur saw every pupil in the room staring at his coat the minute he entered. He saw them wink at one another as he took his seat. He knew his face was turning red, but he opened a book and began to study.

Pretty soon a boy in the seat just behind began to rub Wilbur's velvet collar gently. Then a boy across the aisle reached over and patted his cuff. They were very sly about it. They waited until the teacher's back was turned.

Miss Hixon didn't see the boys, but she had seen the winks and grins. And she meant to do something about it. Suddenly she asked Wilbur if he knew his piece.

"I could say it last night."

"Good! I'd like you to say it this morning. I'm glad you wore your new suit. It looks like one I saw in a fashion magazine. It must have come straight from New York."

"My mother made it."

Then Miss Hixon was really interested. She asked if Mrs. Wright had patterns for the velvet collar and cuffs. She said she'd like to borrow them for her sister.

There wasn't a grin in the room by this time. But Miss Hixon went on: "My sister wants to trim her son's coat with velvet. She said that most boys' winter suits are being made that way. But she'll talk with your mother about it."

There was no more collar-rubbing or cuff-patting. And there wasn't a wink when Wilbur said his piece that afternoon. He didn't forget a single word, and the visitors applauded him.

"I was proud of you," said his mother as they walked home together after the program. "You didn't forget any of that long piece, and I could hear every word."

She looked at Wilbur's suit and added, "I was proud of your suit, too."

Wilbur was thinking so hard that he scarcely heard what his mother was saying. But he was not thinking of either his piece or his suit. There was just one thought in his mind: "I'm glad I faced my classmates—mighty glad."

Any Old Bones Today?

Seven-year-old Orville wanted a larger express wagon. His old wagon was too small for the loads he was hauling now. He had to make many trips to the woodshed every day for wood. If he had a large wagon he could haul enough for the kitchen stove with one trip.

Wilbur agreed. He could use a large wagon for coal when the base-burner was going. That stove just swallowed a bucket of coal.

"And we could haul all the groceries at one time," Orville went on. "A sack of flour and a bushel of peaches and lots of things."

"Muskmelons and watermelons," added Wilbur. "We could get a big load of walnuts next fall."

"There's a large wagon in Martin's store window. It's marked three dollars."

"It might as well be thirty dollars," declared Wilbur. "We haven't any money. I've spent everything I made cutting grass."

"All of it? What did you spend it for?"

"Ice cream. And you helped to eat it."

"Oh, yes, I remember." Then Orville changed the subject quickly. "Wilbur, do you think I could get work cutting grass?"

"You couldn't just now because the grass is all dried up. And it won't grow until we have some rain."

They tried to find other work in their neighborhood but they couldn't. They even went to the grocery and feed store. At each place they were told to come back in a few years.

And still it didn't rain and the new grass didn't

grow. Even the weather was against them. The boys were so discouraged their older brothers felt sorry for them.

One evening Roosh and Lorin told their father they had an idea. They said they had saved a little money, enough to buy the wagon Wilbur and Orvy wanted.

"No," said Mr. Wright firmly. "Your mother and I don't want them to be helped. If we let them alone they'll find a way to buy the wagon. They have always been smart about thinking up things. And they'll do it this time if they know they've got to depend on themselves."

Suddenly the weather changed. A strong breeze began to blow from the east. Wilbur said it would bring rain, it always did.

"An east wind always brings that awful smell from the fertilizer factory too," said Orville. "It's a mile away, but we can smell the fertilizer away over here."

"I guess farmers don't mind the smell. They need the fertilizer for their land."

"Where does the factory get the old bones they grind up to make the fertilizer?"

"I suppose they have to buy them."

"Buy them!" exclaimed Orvy. "I know where there are plenty of old bones."

"So do I! We can make a lot of money."

Some of the Wrights' relatives had always said that Wilbur and Orvy never let any grass grow under their feet. If they had something to do they did it at once. In about two minutes the brothers were on their way to the bone factory.

They hardly noticed the long mile there. And they didn't notice the long mile back at all because of their good luck. The manager had said he would buy all the old bones they could bring.

That afternoon they were picking up old bones from alleys. They hauled them to their back yard and dumped them in a pile. When they had finished this job, they began to ask people for the bones in their back yards.

Everywhere they went they made friends. The lady in the big house said she would save bones for them. She liked them because they were so polite when they asked her.

"You may have all you can find," said the lady in the little house. "Just don't take my dog's bone."

With all these new friends helping, the bone pile was growing larger and larger.

THE BONES HAD DISAPPEARED

In one week they had enough bones to fill the big cart. They decided on Wednesday evening that their first load could be hauled to the factory Thursday.

But Thursday morning the pile wasn't so large as it had seemed the day before. The boys

couldn't understand how they had made such a mistake. Roosh and Lorin were puzzled also.

All day Thursday the boys were hunting for bones. It was harder to find them now. They even took bones away from dogs when the dogs weren't looking. But not from the dog of their friend in the little house. No, indeed!

By Thursday evening the boys were sure their pile was large enough. Their brothers said they would have some left for another load.

Then a strange thing happened. On Friday morning the pile was smaller again. There was no doubt of it. Wilbur said that someone had been stealing them.

"Why would anyone want old bones?" asked Orville.

"To sell. But they let us do the work."

"There are tracks all around the pile," cried Orville. "It rained last night. You can see them plainly."

The others looked and then they laughed. "Dog tracks! Dog tracks!" they shouted.

"There are some over here by the side fence," said Wilbur.

"And by the back fence," said Lorin.

47

"They seem to come from all directions," said Roosh. "From north, south, east and west. The pile of bones was a gold mine for them. And they were smart—they took their gold home with them."

Then the boys decided there were enough bones to fill the cart. But these couldn't be left outside for night visitors.

That evening the cart was loaded and put in the shed. The door was locked and Wilbur kept the key. Saturday morning the bones were still there. Not one was missing.

As soon as breakfast was over the boys started to the fertilizer plant. It was hard work pulling the heavy load that long mile. But they remembered that they would soon have money in their pockets.

They would go to Martin's store on their way back and buy the wagon. They would take it home and give Katie a ride.

An hour or so later their mother saw them coming through the front gate. She knew they had been disappointed. Their faces showed it.

"We didn't get very much," said Orville. "Only twenty cents."

"Is that all?"

"That's all," declared Wilbur. "And it's the last load of bones we'll get."

"The neighbors will be glad. I mean the ones who live just behind us. They came over this morning to complain. They said the wind had been blowing their way for the last week."

"We didn't think of that, did we, Orvy?"

"No, but I know what they meant. It was an east wind."

"We'll have rain soon," said his mother. "Then the grass will begin to grow."

"And then we'll have plenty of work," said Wilbur.

"Grass smells better too," said Orville.

The Farmer and the Cornstalk

IN THE fall of 1878 the Reverend Milton Wright was sent to another state. He had become a bishop and had many new duties. He was needed most in Cedar Rapids, Iowa.

The Wright family had decided to move there. They were on a west-bound train. Their trunks and furniture were in the baggage car ahead. There was also a new express wagon in the baggage car. Wilbur and Orville had bought it with money they had earned.

They were talking about it now as forests, farms and villages rushed by. They wondered what they would use it for in Cedar Rapids.

There would be trips to the grocery of course. People had to eat wherever they went.

Then they talked about their older brothers who were still in Dayton. They were living with relatives and wanted to stay there. Lorin and Roosh liked their high school and wanted to graduate from it. They were both working part-time every day now and made enough to live on.

Besides, there was no telling how long Father would be in Cedar Rapids. He might be sent to another church in a year or so.

Mr. and Mrs. Wright were sitting in the seat facing Orville and Wilbur.

"Well, boys," said their father at last, "we have gone through Ohio and Indiana and part of Illinois. We'll be in Iowa tomorrow morning. And you'll see the tallest corn you ever saw in all your lives."

"How tall?" asked Orville.

Mr. Wright smiled. "That makes me think of

a story about the tall corn in Iowa. Do you want to hear it?"

"Yes! Yes!" cried the others. Katie was stretched out on the seat across the aisle, asleep. She didn't care about corn anyway.

Mr. Wright began: "Well, there was once a young man who owned a big farm in Iowa. His cornfield was so large it took three days to ride through it on horseback. It kept him so busy he didn't have time to go to town except on Saturday. He bought his groceries then. And he bought everything else he needed for the week.

"He always had a good time in town. He visited with friends he met there. There were six of them, all farmers. They also bought their groceries on Saturday, and everything else they would need for the week.

"They told one another about their cattle, horses, colts, mules and pigs. But mostly they talked about their corn and bragged about how

52

fast it was growing. Each one tried to tell a bigger yarn than the others. But Uncle Si White-wash usually came out ahead.

"One Saturday he had said his corn was up to the clouds. He didn't know where it would go from there. It worried him. He was worried about getting the ears too.

" 'I guess I'll have to go up in a balloon,' he said. 'And I'll pick the ears as I float by.'

"Our farmer liked all this fun and didn't want to miss it. But the next Saturday he couldn't get away. He was too busy. But he thought about his friends all morning.

"He wondered if all of them had gone to town. Maybe some were like him, too busy. He'd just like to know what was going on.

"Suddenly he thought of a way to find out. 'Of course!' he said aloud. 'Why didn't I think of that in the first place?'

"He ran to his cornfield and looked about for

the tallest stalk. At last he found one that suited him and began to climb it."

"Climb it!" exclaimed Orvy. "A man can't climb a cornstalk."

"It's just a story," said his mother. "Let your father go on."

"The young man climbed clear to the top. Now he could see for miles and miles. There was the little town as plain as day. It had just one street, but that was empty. No men stood on corners talking. There wasn't anyone in front of the grocery. None of his friends was anywhere in sight.

"But our farmer felt sure that some of them were there. So he turned his head and stretched his neck until he saw what he was looking for.

"'There are Bill Smith and Ed Moore,' he said aloud. 'And there are Sam Long and Dick Rider. There's Lew Hicks. And, bless my soul, there's Uncle Si Whitewash!'"

Orville was puzzled. "You said the street was empty, Father. How could he see his friends?"

"He didn't see them. He saw their horses. They were hitched to the rack in front of the courthouse. He knew every one of them as well as he knew his own."

"Oh!" exclaimed Orville. "I didn't think of that."

Mr. Wright went on: "And now the farmer saw another horse he knew. It was the sheriff's calico mare and it was hitched to a post in front of his office.

"At a rack at the side were tied two other horses. They belonged to the sheriff's two men. So our farmer knew there was no trouble anywhere in the county.

"Just then the sheriff hurried from his office. His two men followed. They jumped on their horses and rode away fast.

"'Robbers!' exclaimed the farmer. 'Or cattle

thieves! Or horse thieves! I'm going to town
to find out. The work will have to wait.' "

WILL HE EVER GET DOWN?

Mr. Wright paused as they passed a little
town. Then he went on with the story.

"He started to climb down. And he climbed
and he climbed but nothing happened. I mean
he wasn't getting any nearer to the ground than
he was when he started."

"Why didn't he jump down?" asked Orville.

"He did think of jumping. But he didn't
dare. He was too high up. The ground was too
far below. And it was getting farther away every minute."

"How could it?" asked Orville. "He was
coming down all the time, wasn't he?"

"He was, but the stalk was growing up all
the time too."

Mrs. Wright laughed. "It doesn't grow that fast in Ohio and Indiana," she said.

"No, indeed! Only Iowa corn grows like lightning, Susan."

"Does it really, Father?" cried Orville. "As fast as lightning?"

"It's a story, silly. Can't you understand that?" asked Wilbur. "It's like 'Jack and the Beanstalk.'"

"Anyway, I want to know how he'll get down."

"The farmer began to worry about that himself. It was like a problem in arithmetic. While he was climbing down one foot the corn was growing up two feet. When would he reach the ground? He couldn't get the answer.

"At last he gave up. He saw he could never make it alone. So he called for help. He called to all his neighbors, north, south, east and west."

"They wouldn't hear him," declared Orville.

"How could they if it took three days to go through his field?"

"He was the best hog caller in the county, son. It was nothing for him to call hogs three miles away. So of course his neighbors heard him. They came at once.

"He begged them to save him. He said he would starve to death up there. And if the night was cold he would freeze.

"The neighbors talked it over. They all liked him and wanted to save him. Some thought he ought to jump even if he broke his legs.

" 'No! No!' cried others. 'He might break his neck!'

"Still others said he might break both."

"Why didn't they get a long ladder?"

"There wasn't a ladder in the county that would be long enough, Orvy. I don't suppose there would be one in the state of Iowa. And they knew it and the young farmer knew it too."

"What did they do?"

"They couldn't think of any way to save him. So they told him good-by and went home."

"Went home!" exclaimed Orville. "How did he get down?"

"That's for you boys to figure out. I want you to tell me how the farmer was saved—if he was."

"I can't make up stories," said Wilbur.

"Neither can I," said Orville.

"Both of you are good at planning how to make things. You don't give up because something is hard to do. You keep on trying till you do it."

"Indeed they do!" said Mrs. Wright.

"Well, this is just another problem. Instead of a clock that won't work, here's a farmer who won't jump. What will you do with him?"

"I'd have him slide down," said Wilbur.

"He couldn't slide over the big leaves. They had been growing fast too, along with the stalk.

I'm afraid your ending won't do, Wilbur. Now, Orvy, it's your turn."

"I think he broke off two big leaves and used them for wings. Then he flew down."

"Good! Good!" exclaimed Mr. Wright. "That's just the way to end that kind of a story."

"It is indeed," agreed Mrs. Wright.

"I should have thought of wings myself," said Wilbur. "You're smart, Orvy."

Then they all curled up on the hard seats and slept. And the train hurried on to the land of tall corn.

Fun and Fear

THE WRIGHT boys were friendly. It didn't take them long to get acquainted with the boys on Adams Street in Cedar Rapids, Iowa.

They were getting acquainted with the city too. Today they had gone to see the rapids in the Cedar River. They were standing on the bank now looking down at the whirling water.

"I wish I could get in it," said Orville. "I'd like to feel that water pushing against my legs. It runs so fast."

"It might knock you down," said his father. "Look how it dashes against the rocks."

"It couldn't throw me down. I'm strong."

"So am I," his father said. "And there's a good woodshed on Adams Street."

"And plenty of willow switches," added Wilbur with a grin.

There was no more trouble about the rapids. Orville always obeyed his father. Besides, he forgot the water when he heard of the Indian camp up the river. The Cedar Rapids boys said it was only two or three miles from town and some of them had been there.

Wilbur and Orville wanted to go, but their parents objected. They said the Indian boys hadn't been coming to their home. They were too polite to go where they hadn't been asked.

So the brothers decided to "play Indian." But they must have war bonnets and Indian drums and arrows. And the way to get them was to make them.

No sooner said than done. It didn't take them long to make a war bonnet. All they had to do was cut a headband from cardboard and glue chicken feathers to it.

But small cardboard drums were a little harder to make, and so were the quivers and arrows.

Their new friends liked the new toys and tried to copy them. But they had to go to the woodshed for help. They weren't used to making things like the two boys from Dayton, Ohio.

At last everything was ready. War bonnets were on heads. Drums and quivers were tied to belts. Then, with bows in hand, away they went to the river.

They went on and on, whooping and laughing and shouting. They didn't stop till they came to the edge of the wood. Here they made a target. This was a square of cardboard nailed onto a big tree.

They began to shoot their arrows. The Iowa boys hit the board but not one of their arrows hit dead center. When Wilbur hit it three times running they were astonished.

Orville thought he should explain. "It's Wilbur's eyes. He could always see farther than the rest of us at home."

Some days they didn't take their bows and arrows. Then they played they were Indian braves, armed with rifles. They attacked settlers in big covered wagons.

"Bang! Bang!" The driver fell.

"Bang! Bang!" The settlers fell.

"Bang! Bang! Bang!" The soldiers came.

Then the braves ran. The drivers and settlers came back to life and were ready for another game.

Sometimes the braves captured the settlers and took them away. And they were never seen again—not for five minutes or so.

The boys didn't know that bright brown eyes were watching them from thick bushes. They didn't dream that a band of big Indian boys was following them every day.

One day the white boys pretended they were on a buffalo hunt. They played they had found tracks and were following them up the riverbank. They had gone quite a distance when they heard fierce yells all about them.

Then a large band of angry Indian boys came running from the woods. They were scowling and shaking their fists and yelling frightfully.

The white boys didn't have a chance to run.

WILBUR THREW—THE CROW FELL

Suddenly a tall Indian boy ran straight to Wilbur. He shook his fists and spoke angrily. "Me—Black Rock! You—make fun—us. No like!"

"No! No! You don't understand," cried Wilbur. "We want to be Indians ourselves. Don't you see our war bonnets?"

Then the Indians laughed. There wasn't a feather on any of their heads.

"No mad," said Black Rock. "Try scare—for fun. Want play—like you. You let?"

Wilbur was surprised but he said of course. Then he asked what they wanted to play.

"Me tell. You—settlers. We—braves. Come quick. Make big noise—shoot—take all you."

Wilbur looked at his friends and they looked at him. They all thought it was a trick. The Indians had planned to seize them and take them to their camp. They shook their heads and Wilbur understood.

He couldn't tell Black Rock they were suspicious. So he said the boys were tired of that game. "Why can't we shoot at a target?" he asked.

"No see bows—no see arrows."

"We'll throw rocks."

"Like throw. Me make target."

He peeled a piece of bark from a tree with his long knife. The others, both Indian and white, brought rocks from the riverbank.

Then the game began. Each one had three throws. Wilbur was the only one to hit dead center. He hit it every time.

Orville was afraid the Indians wouldn't like this. So he hurried to explain again. "It's Wilbur's eyes. He always could see farther than the rest of us at home."

The Indians didn't even listen to him. They were all begging Wilbur to keep on throwing. But he refused. He didn't want to outshine them and maybe make them angry. However, Orville spoiled this. He said that Wilbur could hit a bird flying.

"Show," cried Black Rock. "There—crow!"

"Do you care if I kill it?"

"No care. Crow bad—eat corn." Then Black Rock shook his head. "Can no hit."

The other Indians nodded. Not one thought Wilbur could hit a flying crow. Not many Indians could.

Now Wilbur waited for the crow to fly lower. A rock was in his hand. His keen eyes were on the flying bird. Everyone else watched him. No one spoke.

Suddenly the crow flew a little lower. And

that very instant Wilbur threw. The rock went straight to its mark. The crow fell to the ground!

The Indian boys were delighted. They crowded about Wilbur. They felt his muscles. They praised him so much he was embarrassed. Then they talked to one another in their own language. They were excited and kept pointing to Wilbur.

"What is it?" Orville asked softly. "Why are they pointing to you? Let's run away."

Just then Black Rock turned to Wilbur. "They say want you go our camp. Want braves see. Throw rock—show. Understand?"

Wilbur nodded and smiled. Then Black Rock went on: "Say you good scout for Indians. See enemy far away on plains. See smoke far away in sky."

Then a white man came running from the woods close by. A woman and a girl of six followed him.

"Boys, boys," shouted the man. "I want to talk with you. Don't leave—any of you."

A SPLENDID YOUNG INDIAN

The man now reached the boys. "Who killed that crow?" he asked angrily.

"I did," answered Wilbur politely. "I threw a rock at it."

"It belonged to my little girl. It was her pet."

"Why did you do it?" asked the woman.

"Ned played with me," said the child. Then she began to sob.

Wilbur felt so unhappy he didn't know what to say. But he explained how it had happened. He had thought it was a wild crow flying to some cornfield.

"There are no fields around here," said the man. "There are cabins all through this part of the woods. Didn't you know that?"

"No, sir. We have just moved here."

"Your father will have to pay for the crow. It will cost him five dollars."

"Five dollars!" exclaimed the astonished boy.

"That's what I said."

Now Black Rock spoke to the angry man. "Why you no cut wing? So no fly high. No one shoot then. Me cut wing my crow. He safe— all time safe."

The man didn't answer. He turned to Wilbur and asked where he lived. The boy told him and the man nodded.

"I'll be there in the morning for my money."

Mr. Wright was away on church business. So Wilbur had to tell his mother about the five dollars. "I'll pay it back," he said. "I'll stop school now and get steady work."

"No, Wilbur. We wouldn't let you do that. It wasn't your fault. I'll take the money from our savings."

There was a knock at the front door. "There he is, Mother!"

"I'll give him the money."

When Mrs. Wright opened the door she was surprised. There stood a smiling Indian boy. On his shoulder sat a pet crow. "Crow for you," he said. "No pay—give man—for girl."

By this time Wilbur was at the door. "Black Rock!" he cried. "I can't take your pet."

"Get new crow. Tame—then he pet. Take."

He put the crow on Wilbur's shoulder and left quickly.

That afternoon a little girl in a cabin in the woods was laughing happily. "Look, Mother! Look, Father! This crow is as tame as Ned was. He is beautiful—I love him."

"That's better than five dollars, George. I'm glad you wouldn't take the money from Mrs. Wright."

"I never intended to. I just wanted to scare the boy. But the young Indian was right. It was my fault. I should have clipped Ned's wings."

Orville's Army

THERE WAS to be a great celebration in Cedar Rapids today. It was to honor the completion of the new bridge just above the city. There would be a big parade with soldiers and bands. All stores were closed and school pupils had been dismissed for the morning.

Orville Wright and six other boys managed to get good places on a curb. They yelled until they were hoarse when soldiers marched by. They clapped until they were tired for generals on prancing horses.

Orville took off his hat every time the flag of the United States passed. And so did the new pupil, Jeff Barnes. If the other boys forgot to do this, they received a quick punch from Orville. Then off went their hats too.

Finally the parade was over. It was still too early to go home for dinner. What could they do?

Orville had the answer to that. "Let's have an army of our own," he said. "We can march around and carry flags. Who wants to join?"

They all did. Who would be the general?

"I will," replied Orville. "The rest of you can be colonels. Is that all right?"

It was. But what could they do? An army always did something.

"We're going to the schoolhouse right now," said General Orville Wright. "And we'll march around it and yell and make a lot of noise. Then the janitor will run out and chase us away."

The colonels began to laugh. Suddenly they stopped. They said the janitor would tell the principal and he would tell their teacher. And she would keep them in after school for a whole week.

"I didn't think of that part. We'll do something else."

Just then Wilbur called from across the street and motioned to Orville to come. He went at once but he said he'd be back in just a minute.

"Will he really think up something?" asked the new pupil.

"He always does," replied Alfred. "His head is full of ideas all the time. My father said it is because Orvy is always planning a way to make things."

"My mother thinks that too," declared Eugene. "She said Orvy's mind is working all the time. Not just part of the time like mine."

The others laughed. And at least four confessed that their parents had the same idea about Orville Wright.

"Well, everyone can't make things like Wilbur and Orvy," said one.

"What does Orville make?" asked Jeff.

"Oh, wooden tops, whistles, slingshots and such things," replied Roy. "Last week he and his brother made peashooters to sell. They gave a box of paper wads with each one, free."

"I can tell you what they are doing now," said Eugene. "They are making a harness for their goat."

"Will they hitch it to their new wagon?" asked George.

"No, indeed! They are afraid the goat will jam it against something. And it certainly would. They are making a wagon themselves for that goat to pull."

"It's about finished," Paul told them. "Orvy is looking for wheels. He asked Mother yesterday if she had an old baby buggy. He said that the front wheels would be just right."

Just then Orville came back. He was grinning from ear to ear and his eyes were shining. "I've got a great idea!" he cried. "Listen! We'll capture Wilbur. He'll be working in the woodshed till noon—he just told me. We'll make him surrender!"

"How?" asked the colonels.

"There are wide cracks on each side of the door. We'll shoot paper wads through them. And we'll keep it up till he surrenders. Then we'll laugh at him."

The army was delighted. It would be funny to see old Wilbur come out with his hands up. They'd laugh their heads off. But what about peashooters for the wads? If they went home their mothers wouldn't let them leave before dinner.

"I have enough for all of you and enough wads too. Come on! There's no time to lose."

General Wright halted his army at his own

front gate. "Listen!" he ordered. "We've got to creep up on Wilbur and take him by surprise. If he sees us he'll play some trick. So don't make any noise while I'm inside."

The colonels hardly had time to whisper before their general came back. He brought the arms and ammunition and passed them out. Then he led his army to the woodshed.

They crept up quietly but there was a mixup at the door. The general had placed two left-handed colonels at the crack on the right side. It took a little whispering to straighten this out, but not much. No one thought Wilbur heard it.

But Wilbur's ears were as keen as his eyes. He had heard the whispering and at this very moment was peeping out, through a crack. He guessed what the boys were up to.

"Surrender!" called General Orvy Wright. "Surrender, or we'll shoot!"

"Shoot!" shouted Wilbur.

Now paper pellets were shot through cracks. Wilbur couldn't dodge them, they came so fast. It was like being hit with hailstones. Then the attack stopped.

"You may as well admit that you're defeated. You haven't a chance. Open the door and come on out!" shouted General Wright.

"*No!* Never!"

"Then we'll keep shooting!"

"Go on!"

The general handed out more ammunition. The colonels stuffed it in their pockets and prepared to attack again.

"Get ready, take aim, fire!" came the command from General Wright.

Suddenly a long pole was thrust out from the space under the door. It moved back and forth until the army was mowed down. The general and the soldiers were all tangled up together in a heap on the ground.

Wilbur opened the door. "Surrender your-
selves!" he shouted. Then it was his turn to
laugh, for the army got up quickly and ran.

The following afternoon, after school, the army went to Goose Creek to swim. When the soldiers were tired of swimming they built a dam. Their general said it would be fun to see the water back up against it and get higher and higher.

They didn't make the dam across the wide creek. That would be too much work. It was built across the little stream flowing into the creek, but not right where they met. Orville chose a place some distance away where the land was level. He said it would be easier to work there.

It didn't take long to make a wall with rocks and brush. They plastered it with mud to make it hold together. It was only a foot high but it reached from shore to shore.

They couldn't wait to watch the water back up. It was late and they had to go home. They would come out tomorrow afternoon to see how much water was back of the dam.

When the boys came back they were amazed. The water behind the dam was level with it. And it had spread over the low land on each side. It looked like a little lake.

They were delighted. They looked and looked. They talked and talked. And all the time there was something happening behind them.

Four Indian squaws had come out of the wood. Their moccasins made no noise as they came closer and closer. Soon they were near enough to touch the boys.

Then they shouted suddenly, "Hi! Hi!"

The boys turned quickly. They were frightened at the scowling faces they saw.

"You make dam?" asked the oldest squaw sharply.

"We just made it for fun," said Orville in a weak little voice.

"Fun!" she snapped. "For fun spoil garden!"

"Garden! We didn't know—we didn't notice any plants."

"Why no see? Beans up."

"I guess we just thought it was grass. We are all sorry."

The boys nodded their heads gravely. But the squaws still scowled.

The same one spoke again. "Land belongs us—plant seed. Now beans rot. Too wet. Must plant new. Much work. No like."

The older women nodded and made angry sounds.

"You make dam," the oldest went on. "Now you break. Carry rocks off. Carry brush off. Quick!"

The frightened boys took off their shoes. They rolled their pants shorter. They had started to remove their shirts when the squaw stopped them.

86

"No time that!" she cried. "Rain come soon. Go now!"

The boys didn't argue with her. They waded into the stream at once and began to break down the dam.

They carried wet rocks and muddy brush from the creek and threw it over the bank. They made trip after trip. And all the time those angry

eyes were watching them. The boys worked as fast as they could. Tearing the dam down wasn't nearly as much fun as building it had been.

At last they finished. Then the old squaw shook a finger at them. "No make more dam here," she said. "You no beavers. Go!"

They went. And the minute they were out of sight the army disbanded. Each boy ran to his own home as fast as he could.

But the war wasn't over. There was another battle on the home front. It began when their mothers saw those muddy clothes. And it went on and on until the whole story was told—the army—the dam—the squaws—everything.

Of course the six mothers of the six colonels blamed their general. They said that Orville Wright thought up too many things. He was too daring. He would lead all the boys into trouble. And they would follow him like so many sheep. If he tried to fly from the barn roof they would be silly enough to try it too. And all of them would break their necks.

The general's mother didn't say much but she did something. She made Orville wash his muddy clothing all by himself. And this cured General Wright of army life. He didn't want any more of it.

A Toy That Flew

THE WRIGHTS' neighbors in Cedar Rapids were exactly like those in Dayton about noise. They said they expected growing boys to make some when they played in their back yards. But they didn't have to whoop and groan as the Wright brothers were doing now.

Why all this groaning anyway? It was something new. They looked out their kitchen doors and saw something new themselves. Wilbur and Orville were tossing a small object up into the air. And if it didn't sail away just like a balloon! But it wasn't a balloon.

What was it? An object couldn't fly. They'd

have to find out about this. They hurried to the Wright yard.

Mr. and Mrs. Wright came from the house and everybody watched the boys. They saw Wilbur toss the object up, and at once there were cries and shouts of surprise: "Look! Look! It is flying! It is flying!"

Then the tiny thing fell and everyone groaned, visitors, parents and boys.

"It can't stay up very long," said Mrs. Wright. "It hasn't the power."

"It's wonderful that it stays up at all," old Mr. Benton declared. "As old as I am, I have never seen anything like it. And I have been interested in inventions for years."

"It was made by a Frenchman," Mr. Wright explained.

"He must be a great scientist. He knew how to give this little toy the power to fly. It is a wonderful invention."

"They called it a *helicopter* in Chicago where I bought it."

"*Helicopter*, eh? I must find out about this Frenchman. I must learn whether he is the first to make such a toy."

Wilbur brought the toy to the visitors. They handled it carefully as they examined it. They noticed the light frame of cork and bamboo. They talked about the two tiny paper fans and the two rubber bands.

"The bands were twisted," Wilbur pointed out. "Maybe that has something to do with making it fly."

"Maybe it has," said his father. "They pull the fans and make them whirl."

"They whirl fast," said Orville.

The neighbors had to go now. They thanked the boys for letting them see their wonderful flying toy. They said they had never expected to see anything fly but birds.

Mr. Benton thought the boys would be playing with their toy the next day and he watched for them. But he was disappointed. Two days passed without his seeing them. On the third day he went to the house and asked to look at the toy.

"Oh!" exclaimed Wilbur. "I meant to tell you, Mr. Benton, but I forgot. The toy won't fly. It's broken. Both fans are torn. I guess it just wore out."

"We played with it too much," Orville added.

"But I'm going to make one," Wilbur told him. "I remember how it looked. It won't be hard to copy."

"I'm glad you will try, Wilbur, but you won't find it easy. In fact, I'll be surprised if you succeed."

After Mr. Benton left, Wilbur wondered what he meant by being surprised. "Of course I can make it!" he declared. "Of course I can!"

The cork, bamboo, thin paper and rubber bands would cost a good deal, more than Wilbur could pay. He had a little money from the sale of the peashooters. But his share, one-half, wasn't enough to buy all this material.

Orville offered his half, but Wilbur refused to take it. He said that Orvy couldn't help him with this kind of work. He would have to measure and figure. Orvy was too young for that; he was only nine and a half. No, it wouldn't be fair to use his money. Wilbur would have to give it up until he could make enough.

One of the neighbors heard about Wilbur's decision and was indignant. She went straight to the Reverend Milton Wright himself.

She told him he ought to give his son enough money to buy the material he needed. It was wonderful that a boy of thirteen or so would even want to make such a toy.

"He might become an inventor," she said.

"I hope he will, Mrs. Strong. That is the very reason I cannot help him. He will never invent anything worth while unless he learns to depend on himself."

"Oh, of course he would have to do his own thinking. I was talking about giving him money."

"The two go together. If he really wants to make that toy he'll find a way to buy the materials that he needs."

He was right. In a few days Wilbur had started a new business and Orville was his partner. They were making money on their goat and wagon.

They charged five cents to ride in the wagon and drive the goat. They charged three cents to ride and have the goat led. They did a big business from the start. But after two weeks they had to give it up.

The goat ruined the neighbors' gardens with her sharp hoofs. She chased their dogs and cats. She butted their children. She pulled down their clotheslines on washday.

Finally Mr. Wright gave her to a friend who lived in the country. The boys hated to lose their pet, but, thanks to Nanny, Wilbur had enough to buy the materials.

He had decided to make his toy larger than the Chicago toy. He would make it twice the size. He'd make the fans twice the size of the other fans.

This would give it twice the power and it should fly twice as long. Didn't his father and Mr. Benton think that it would?

Both men said it sounded all right. But they weren't scientists. They couldn't say it would turn out that way. Wilbur would have to try it out.

Orville watched his brother work every

chance he had. He saw him measure, figure, cut out and glue. He noticed how very careful he was with the thin paper. He was amazed at the light touch of Wilbur's fingers.

At last the toy was finished and the neighbors came over to see the test. Everyone was hoping it would be successful.

Wilbur was excited. The hand that held the toy was trembling. His mother and father noticed how pale he was. Suddenly he straightened up and lifted his arm for the throw.

"Look!" he cried. "It's going!"

He tossed the toy up into the air. It didn't fly at all. It fell at once and Orville picked it up. Wilbur was so disappointed he couldn't speak to anyone. Mr. Wright and Mr. Benton examined the toy.

"I can't see anything wrong with it," said Mr. Wright thoughtfully. "The fans and rubber bands are in place."

"Yet something is wrong," declared Mr. Benton. "Something is very wrong."

"It might be the fans," Wilbur suggested. "Maybe two weren't enough for this toy. It's twice the size of that other one. It should have had twice as many fans. Don't you think that was the trouble, Father?"

"It could be, son. It sounds reasonable. What do you think, Mr. Benton?"

"As you say, it sounds reasonable. But I do not know. If I did, I would make one myself. The toy obeys a law of science. Find this law and you'll know the answer to your question, Wilbur. Nothing else can tell you."

"Flying Fiddlesticks!"

In 1881 the schools of Richmond, Indiana, had three new pupils named Wright, two brothers and a sister. Their father was the preacher for a new church. The family had moved from Iowa about one month before.

Wilbur Wright, age fourteen, was in the high school. Orville Wright, ten, was in the sixth year of the grade school. Their sister, Katherine, seven, was in grade two and was getting along fine.

So were Wilbur and Orville. They were already at the head of their arithmetic classes, just as they had been in Cedar Rapids. Their teachers said they seemed to love arithmetic problems and the harder the better.

Some of their classmates couldn't understand this. They said those Wright boys must be queer. The idea of liking hard problems!

Wilbur was making splendid grades in English also. The English teacher said he had read more good books than any pupil in her classes.

"He remembers them too," she told Mr. Wright. "He doesn't forget the smallest thing. It's just as if he had a camera in his head. Every page makes a picture in his mind."

The minister was pleased. He told his wife about it as soon as he got home. "Now I have a son who takes after me," he said with a smile. "I have always loved to read good books."

Susan smiled. "And Wilbur hates to put one down as much as you."

"I wish he had more time for reading. I wish I had time to help him with his chores."

There were too many chores to suit Wilbur. He had grass to cut in the summer, leaves to rake in the fall, weeds to pull in the spring and snow to shovel in the winter. Coal and wood had to be carried in and ashes carried out.

Of course Orville helped, and of course both wagons were used for hauling. They were thankful they had brought them from Cedar Rapids. They could finish their chores in half the time.

They were thankful for another thing also. Their mother paid them for extra work, like hauling apples from an orchard, or picking cherries and blackberries.

This gave them money for their baseball bats, mitts and balls. Both boys were on teams and were practicing for a big game. They didn't even have time to build anything new.

Wilbur had bought material for another flying toy but he hadn't touched it. The days weren't long enough for everything.

But when spring came and the days were longer he lost no time. One day he took his material for the toy to the woodshed. In five minutes he took it back to the house. His mother said it was too cold for him to work out there.

She told him to use the dining-room table as long as he needed it. The family would eat in the kitchen. Mr. Wright agreed with her. He was eager to see if the four fans would make the toy fly.

Wilbur was sure that they would. He was so sure he whistled and sang while he worked. By the third day he had made a good start. Then he had to stop, or he thought he did.

An old friend of Mrs. Wright's came for a visit. She was Miss Minnie Newcomb and she had brought two large valises. Wilbur felt ill when he saw them. He knew what the valises meant. She would stay a long time, two or three weeks anyway. She always did.

They would have to eat in the dining room now. He'd have to stop work on his flying toy. It was hard luck, but he'd have to be nice to company.

He was taking his things from the table when Mrs. Wright stopped him. "You needn't do

that," she said. "We will eat in the kitchen. You won't mind, will you, Minnie?"

"Oh, no, indeed!" replied the lady with a sour smile. "I don't mind at all. Of course we never do at home. But don't let me change your plans. I see Wilbur is using the table."

"Yes," said the minister firmly, "Wilbur will be using the table all this week."

SHE SAID THAT ONLY A BIRD COULD FLY

Susan tried to explain later on. "It won't do to stop Wilbur's work now, Minnie. He might lose his interest."

"Is his work so important?"

"It's the most important thing in the world to him. If he succeeds it may become important to everyone. It's an invention——"

Miss Newcomb interrupted. "It's another bean huller, I suppose. The country is full of them. He's wasting his time. Well, of course it's none of my business, Susan. But you and Milton are spoiling that boy. If he were my son he wouldn't have all that trash on my dining-room table."

Susan smiled. "Everything there is precious to him, even the old rags."

"But you let him melt glue on your kitchen stove—while you were getting dinner too!"

"He needed it then. He couldn't wait."

"He would have to wait in my house. And he couldn't drive me out of my dining room."

"This is his home," said Susan gently. "We feel he has the right to use any part of it."

Miss Newcomb paid no attention to this. She went on to say that Orvy had been tracking mud into the kitchen all morning.

Mrs. Wright smiled and said that Orvy was making flour paste and was afraid it would boil over. "He is making a kite," she added.

"Kites! Bean hullers! They are busy, aren't they? Do they carry on like this all the time?"

"I think they would if it weren't for school and baseball. But, Minnie, Wilbur isn't making a bean huller. He is working on a flying toy."

"I've never heard of such a thing. What is it?"

Susan explained, but Miss Newcomb wouldn't believe one word. "You only *thought* the Frenchman's toy flew. But it was really floating like pinwheels children make and toss up."

"No, indeed! It flew all by itself, and under its own power. A dozen people saw it."

"Oh, come now, Susan! You know better than that. Nothing on this earth can fly all by itself except a bird."

"Wait till Wilbur finishes his '*bird*.' You'll see something fly all by itself. He thinks he can test it Friday."

Early Friday morning, as soon as breakfast was over, the family and their guest went out on the front porch. They watched Wilbur toss his new toy up into the air. Then they saw the failure. The toy fell at once.

Everyone but Miss Newcomb was surprised. They had been sure the four fans would lift it and carry it along. Wilbur was terribly upset. His hands trembled as he picked up the toy.

"What's the matter with it?" asked Orville. "You measured every piece of it."

"Wilbur," said his father, "I am sure now that Mr. Benton was right. The Frenchman built his toy according to some law of science. You will have to find that law before you try to make another."

"And when you do you'll make one that will fly," declared his mother. "I know you will."

"It can't be done, Wilbur," said Miss Newcomb. "It's against the law of nature. If a heavy thing goes up, it's bound to fall down. Flying toys! Humph! Flying fiddlesticks!"

The Brave Money-Makers

WILBUR couldn't spend any more time on inventions. He was working all day on Saturdays. He wanted to pay for his schoolbooks this term. They cost a good deal, especially his science book. He had found work in a machine shop.

He liked to work with machinery. He liked it so much he decided he wouldn't quit when he had paid for his books, if his boss wanted him. His boss did want him. He said Wilbur was one of his best workmen.

"That boy thinks everything out before he does it. He isn't careless with the machinery.

When he uses a tool he puts it back where he found it. He'll make a first-class mechanic."

Orville was busy making kites; not one or two, but a dozen. They were to sell and they were ready now, all but the tails. It wouldn't take long to fasten them to the frames.

He needed money to buy a doll for Katie's birthday in August. He had spent the last of his peashooter and goat-rides money. He had bought a stuffed owl from his new friend Gansey Johnston. Mrs. Johnston had thrown it away because it was moth-eaten.

Orville wished he hadn't bought it. His mother wouldn't let him keep it in his room on account of the moths. And its feathers were dropping out. Its head was almost bald.

It stood on a shelf now in the woodshed. Orville had stretched out its wings. He thought it looked wonderful. "It makes me want to fly, myself," he told Wilbur.

110

"That's just the way I feel, Orvy, every time I look at it. I'm glad you bought it."

"I'll make enough on kites to buy the doll. I'll have them ready to sell by Saturday."

But Friday night it turned cold. Saturday there was a cold drizzle. It wasn't kite weather. And the weather stayed bad for days. No one wanted a kite and no one bought a kite.

Katie's birthday would be next week, August nineteenth. It would be Orville's birthday too, but of course they weren't the same age. Katie would be eight. He would be eleven.

His mother said she wouldn't change their birthdays if she could. One dinner always did for both and so did one cake. But she always baked an extra large one. And Katie always gave Orville a gift and he always gave one to her. She'd feel bad if he didn't.

Mother made Katie's gifts to him. She would knit something for his gift to his sister too. But

he knew Katie wanted another doll. He ought to earn enough for a small one, say twenty-five cents, at least.

However, he hadn't been able to sell his kites. He sat in the woodshed and looked at the fine kites he had made. But there wasn't much use in looking at them. If nobody would buy them, they weren't any good to him.

He couldn't find any extra work to do either. He worried and worried about earning some money. He talked about it one night to Wilbur.

"Oh, you'll think up something," Wilbur said. "You thought of our bone business. Just keep your eyes open."

He did, and in two days he was in a new business. He was picking up scrap iron from alleys and gutters. He would sell it to the junk yard man as soon as he had enough to fill his large wagon.

Katie was determined to help him. She said

she needed money too. She wanted to buy something for someone. So Orville made her a partner. She was to get half of all they made.

She was delighted. She went about knocking at back doors and asking ladies if they had any old iron. She said her brother would haul it away. Everyone gave her something. They all liked the friendly little girl. In a week's time there was quite a pile of scrap iron in the Wright's back yard.

"It's a fine business," Orville said. "The neighbors can't smell it and their dogs can't eat it."

Early Saturday morning he loaded his large wagon. He was careful not to make much noise because he didn't want Katie to hear him. She wanted to go with him, but he told her he didn't need her. He could haul it alone.

Orville was afraid to take Katie to the junk yard. It was in a bad part of town. Wilbur had

114

told him that and Wilbur knew. He worked near the yard in Ball's Machine Shop.

Orville was hurrying along when he heard Katie calling him. There she was, running to catch up. He waited, and when she came he scolded her a little. "I told you not to come, Kate. The junk yard is in a part of town where little girls shouldn't go."

"I was afraid the man wouldn't give you my part of the money."

"Of course he will. Did you ask Mother if you could go?"

"I didn't have time, Orvy. I wanted to catch up with you."

"Oh, all right, come along. It isn't much farther, but it's dirty and dusty."

The sidewalk ended soon and they had to walk in the road. It was rough with deep ruts. Orville could hardly pull the wagon over them. At last he let his sister help. It was hard work for both. The ruts became deeper and the road rougher. After a while they had to stop to rest.

They sat on the step of an old tumble-down shed. The wagon was at their feet. Orville pointed to Ball's Machine Shop. "There it is, on the corner of the alley. It has a red door. Do you see it?"

"Yes. It's a pretty door. Let's go to see Willie."

"We'll stop on the way back. We'd better go on now."

Just then a rock bounced off the wagon. There was a rattle of iron as pieces on the top of the load fell to the ground. Another rock hit the wagon and more pieces fell.

The children jumped up and looked about. The rock thrower was in the alley. He was picking up another rock.

"Get back, Kate!" cried Orville. "Stay behind me! Watch out for the rocks!"

116

The strange boy ran from the alley and came straight toward the children. He was all of fifteen and he was rough-looking and dirty.

Orville wasn't used to mean boys. But he knew he was seeing one now. He was too angry to be frightened. "What do you mean throwing rocks at my wagon?" he shouted.

"It's not your wagon any more," said the boy. "It's mine. I'm taking that iron to the junk yard. Let go of the handle!"

"I won't let go! Take your hands off my arm!"

The bully pulled Orville away from the wagon and threw him down. In an instant Orville was on his feet and ready to fight. He doubled up his fists and struck out. He was no match for the older and stronger boy. He was knocked down again. This time he couldn't get up.

The thief started away with the wagon. Then that red door on the corner opened. Out came Wilbur and two other workmen! Behind them came Katherine.

"There he is!" she shouted. "In the alley—with our wagon!"

118

Wilbur hurried to his brother.   The other two hurried after the thief. "Stop! Stop!" they called.

The boy left the wagon and ran. The men ran after him. The boy was climbing over a fence when they caught him. He tried to get away but they held him tight.

"Well, well, if it isn't Pete again!" exclaimed one. "You are always trying to get something for nothing, aren't you?"

"I didn't steal it! I was just hauling it away for him."

"You can't tell us a story like that," said one. "We know you too well."

"Come along to the shop," said the other. "We'll send word to your father."

By this time Wilbur had Orville on his feet. And Orville was saying he felt all right now. He was going on to the junk yard with the iron.

"I'm going with you," said Kate.

"I'm going with both of you," declared their older brother. "And this is your last trip down here alone if I have anything to say about it."

Wilbur had a good deal to say that evening. His parents listened and they agreed with him.

"There are to be no more trips to that junk yard unless I am with you," said Mr. Wright firmly.

"I don't think we are going again," said Orville. "We got only ten cents for the load."

"We can't buy any presents," said Katherine. She seemed about ready to cry. Orvy looked sad too.

Mrs. Wright said the birthday cake would do for their gifts to each other.

Then some neighbors came to ask about Orvy. They had heard about the bully. And they were glad Orvy hadn't been hurt.

They all bragged about Katherine. Wasn't she smart to run to the machine shop? And wasn't she brave to go on to the junk yard? My! My!

"She wanted her money," explained Orville. "She was afraid the man wouldn't give it to me."

The neighbors laughed. Then they bragged about Orville. Wasn't he a brave one to try to fight that bully? And then to go on to the junk yard after he'd been hurt! My! My! That took courage.

"He wanted his money, too," explained Wilbur with a smile.

Everyone laughed and then the neighbors went home.

The Wright and Johnston Circus

THE Barnum and Bailey Circus had come and gone a week ago. But the Richmond children were still talking about the tigers, leopards, elephants and hyenas.

Wilbur couldn't forget the way the clown walked on stilts. It was the funniest thing he had ever seen. Finally he made up his mind to try it. He was making himself a pair of stilts.

He was too busy to pay much attention to Orvy's talk about getting up a circus of their own. They would call it The Wright Brothers' Circus.

"You have to have live animals, Orvy."

"We can have stuffed ones. Gansey Johnston's father has a lot of stuffed birds and animals. There is a big grizzly bear among them—and a wolf! Mr. Johnston stuffed them all himself. He said he liked to do this."

Wilbur was becoming interested. He asked where the show would be given. Their woodshed wasn't large enough.

"Mr. Johnston said we could have it in his barn. Gansey wants to help, but we don't know a thing we can do except turn somersaults and do handsprings."

"Barnum and Bailey had a play about Buffalo Bill last year. This year they had one about Little Red Riding Hood."

"That's what we'll do! We've got a stuffed wolf for her. And we can pretend the grizzly bear is a buffalo for Buffalo Bill. What do you think?"

"It sounds all right. But you'll have to advertise to get a crowd. I'll write a notice for you. How many stuffed birds are there?"

"Six. And there is my owl—it still has some feathers."

Wilbur wrote the advertisement that evening. This is what he said:

WRIGHT AND JOHNSTON CIRCUS!

Coming! August Third!
Greatest Show on Earth!
Wright and Johnston Sole Owners!
Magnificent! Mammoth! Colossal!
    Amazing!
Thousands of Strange Birds from
    Strange Lands!
Little Red Riding Hood and a Wolf!
Buffalo Bill and Buffalo!
Fierce Grizzly Bear!
Tumblers and Clown!
Drummers and Drums!

FREE PARADE

Led by W. & J. on Iron Horses!
At 1:00 P.M.—Down First Street
    and Up Second Street!

At 2:00 P.M.—Johnston's Barn!
Tickets—Five Cents Each!
No Adults!

There was no money to pay for the advertisement. This didn't bother the Wright brothers. They sent the notice to the newspaper by mail. Mrs. Johnston said the paper wouldn't print it because it wasn't news.

"But it is news," Mr. Johnston declared. "I think it's big news when boys as young as Orvy and Gansey are smart enough to get up a circus. It shows they know how to plan things."

"Well, yes, that is true."

"It is also news," Mr. Johnston went on, "when a boy of sixteen can write such an advertisement as Wilbur wrote. It sounds as good as the Barnum and Bailey posters. I hope the paper will print every word of it."

Of course the Wrights hoped so too. They hurried to look at their paper in the morning and there it was. Right above it was a line the newspaper had added: *What Are the Boys Up To?*

A thousand persons saw this line and then read Wilbur's notice. And a thousand persons smiled and said they were going to see for themselves.

So on August third at 1:00 P.M., First and Second Streets were crowded. Whole families were trying to find a good place to see the parade. There were almost as many as there had been for the Barnum and Bailey Circus parade.

The Wright and Johnston parade was on time too. At one o'clock on the dot people heard the rat-tat-tat of drums. It was coming!

The parade was led by Wright and Johnston on "Iron Horses," as advertised. Their horses didn't prance but they were just as hard to manage as if they did. They were high-wheel bicycles. The "Sole Owners" were a sight to see. Gold paper stars glittered on their white shirts.

Red, white and blue paper ribbons fluttered from their white paper caps, and from the handlebars of their "horses." Everyone clapped.

Three drummer boys followed. They wore green paper caps with high crowns. They looked straight ahead and beat their drums hard, fast and loud.

The "thousands of strange birds" came next— seven stuffed birds fastened to a plank. This was carried by two boys who were to see the show free.

Katie Wright followed. She was Little Red Riding Hood and wore a red cape and red hood. Of course the stuffed wolf followed her. It had been tied in a wagon and looked very fierce, standing up with its mouth wide open.

The boy who pulled the wagon tried to howl like a wolf. People seemed to like this, for they laughed and clapped their hands. One man shouted, "Fine! Fine!"

The people laughed again when Corky Johnston came along. He was Gansey's younger brother, age nine. He wore his father's high boots and his grandmother's shawl. His mother's fur scarf was around his neck. His grandfather's big black hat was on his head.

False whiskers were glued to his chin. His cheeks were painted a bright red. No one had to ask who he was. He carried a large sign:

> I am Buffalo Bill!
> I'll Shoot a Buffalo at the Show!

128

"I'm coming!" shouted boys on sidewalks. And they cheered and clapped their hands.

Close behind came the big, brown stuffed bear with mouth open and long teeth showing. It was in a cart pulled by another "free" helper. It scared the youngest children.

They soon forgot the bear, for next came a beautiful pony led by her boy master. Then came four handsome dogs led by their boy masters. Everyone applauded.

Then the parade turned into an alley and headed for Johnston's barn.

THE GREATEST SHOW ON EARTH

The big barn was filled in a few minutes. Boys and girls sat on the clean floor. They watched the back door of the barn closely. The actors would use this. They were out in the barnyard now.

As many more children waited outside in the house yard for the second show. The ticket seller had said there would be one. He ought to know. He was Orville Wright's brother Wilbur.

Now the drummers drummed and the show began. Through the back door came the "Sole

Owners," Wright and Johnston, in their fancy clothes. They took off their caps with the ribbon streamers and gave them to a helper.

Then the two boys turned somersaults, and they were experts. The audience applauded from the beginning. But when Wright and Johnston did handsprings, the audience went wild. They would hardly let the boys stop.

Finally the boys ran out and Little Red Riding Hood came in. A wolf howled outside.

"I'm scared," she said. "That wolf is after me! I wish I had a place to hide. Oh, here it comes! And I can't get away! Oh! Oh! Oh!—I'll stay close to the door."

Wright and Johnston came in now. They were pulling the wagon in which the stuffed wolf was tied. Wright did the talking for the wolf and Johnston did the howling.

"Go away! Go away!" cried the girl. "I'm afraid of you!"

"Don't run from me, child. I am your dear grandmother," said Wright.

"My dear grandmother doesn't have whiskers."

"Oh, I just pasted them on for fun. Come closer and you'll see."

"No! No! Grandma's voice wasn't like yours. I have never heard her howl."

"I have a bad cold and I am very hoarse. Come closer so I can speak more softly."

Little Red Riding Hood went close to the wagon. She gave the wolf one look. Then she ran back to the door.

"What's the matter now?" asked the wolf.

"I saw your feet! Grandma doesn't have claws."

"I'm hungry! I won't wait any longer. I'm coming after you!"

Johnston howled. Red Riding Hood screamed. Then Wright and Johnston began to pull the wagon toward the little girl.

"Run! Run!" cried a little girl in the audience. "The wolf will eat you!"

Red Riding Hood laughed. Johnston stopped howling and laughed. Everyone laughed. Then Kate put her hand on the wolf's stuffed head and they went away together.

The children loved this act. They clapped and clapped till they were tired. Then they waited for the next act. They waited and waited.

It was time for Buffalo Bill to go on. But Buffalo Bill refused to go through with it. He said he couldn't stand his hot clothes any longer.

"Look at this fur around my neck!" yelled Corky. "I'm nearly smothered to death. You made me wear it."

"It won't hurt you to wear it five minutes longer," said Gansey.

"It will too! And these boots hurt my feet. They are too large. You made me wear them."

"You don't have to walk," said Orville. "You can stand still and shoot at the buffalo. Look, Corky, I've got this grizzly bear all ready for you. And here's your peashooter!"

"Shoot it yourself!" shouted Corky. "I'm tired of being Buffalo Bill, and I don't want to be in your old circus." Then he ran away.

The partners didn't know what to do. They might have had a clown go in and do funny things, but their clown hadn't arrived. He had got scared at the last minute.

Then Wilbur offered to help them. He said he would walk on his stilts. He had them with him. He had walked over on them.

The "Sole Owners" were pleased. They told the drummers to drum while Wilbur was getting ready. Then they made his face white with flour paste. They put Katherine's red hood on his head. They put her red cape over his shoulders.

Then he climbed onto his stilts and went into the barn. The partners heard so much applause they went in themselves. Wilbur was doing funny tricks on his stilts and the audience was delighted. They laughed, clapped, whistled and cheered. They made so much noise no one heard what was going on outside.

Corky was out there getting even for his sore feet. He had taken off his hot costume and had

climbed to the roof of a low shed. He stood there now calling down to the children who were waiting outside the barn.

"Listen!" he shouted. "There won't be any second show! You can go home now! Go home!"

Of course they left. They thought he had been told to say that there wouldn't be a second show.

But Wright and Johnston didn't care. They had made enough—two dollars and thirty cents! That was one dollar and fifteen cents for each partner. They hadn't dreamed they would make so much. It surely had been the greatest show on earth for them, Gansey said.

"And the most magnificent, mammoth and colossal," added Orville.

"Rats!" shouted Corky from the shed roof.

In and Out
of Trouble

IT WAS Wilbur's act in the Wright and Johnston Circus that started the stilt craze in Richmond. By the time a week had passed, several boys had made stilts and were learning to use them.

Orville and Gansey were working on theirs. Wilbur was helping them. He showed them how to make foot rests and where to fasten them to the poles. He told them to cut leather foot straps from an old shoe and nail them above the rests.

The boys didn't want straps. They said they didn't need them.

"Then you'll have to lift your poles with your

hands every step you take. Look! I'll show you," said Wilbur.

The boys saw the difference at once and followed Wilbur's advice. In two days they could walk without falling.

Then the craze struck Kate and Corky. Mrs. Wright and Mrs. Johnston consented and Wilbur went to work. He brought strong poplar poles from the woods. He measured the children's height. He cut the poles the right length for each. Then he planed and polished the poles until they shone like satin.

He fastened the foot rests at exactly the right height for them. The foot straps fitted their feet. He took pains to make every part exactly right.

When they were finished both Kate and Corky were delighted. They went about showing them off before they had learned to walk.

From then on boys and girls came begging

Wilbur to make stilts for them. Their parents had told them to ask him, they said. And they would pay whatever he charged. Yes, indeed, they would bring old shoes for straps.

It didn't take Wilbur long to decide. He wasn't working in the machine shop just now. He had been laid off until fall. He needed a new suit before school opened. And there were no more hand-me-downs from Roosh and Lorin. Certainly he would make stilts.

The business boomed. He had more customers than he could take care of. Every one of them brought shoes for straps. Mothers said they had to watch their good shoes like hawks. Fathers said they had to sleep in theirs.

Before long the stilt walkers were all over town. They were all over the sidewalks too. They tried to be careful, but several small children were knocked down and hurt. Walkers themselves were hurt.

Grownups began to walk in the streets. Drivers of wagons and carriages complained. Everyone complained. But the stilts went on.

Then school opened and the principal laid down the law. Stilts were not to be brought to school yards or buildings. If any were found, they would be kept by the principal until the end of the term.

This ended the craze and people were thankful. Wilbur the stiltmaker was glad too. He had bought his new suit. And there was enough left over for schoolbooks. He didn't need anything more. Besides, he had to study.

HALLOWEEN FUN AND FALSE FACES

It was Halloween, and Orville and Gansey were ready to go out. They had bought the ugliest false faces they could find. Their stilts were on the front porch.

141

But Mr. Wright put his foot down. He said it would be dangerous to wear masks while on stilts. They could take their choice. It was either stilts or masks.

The boys looked so unhappy Mrs. Wright offered to paint their faces. She said she could make them look uglier than their masks.

She used red candy, bluing and white flour paste. She made them look like painted Indians on the war path. Wilbur was so delighted he had his face painted too.

Then these three frightful creatures climbed onto their stilts and went down the street whooping. People got out of their way in a hurry. Even dogs ran barking in terror.

The three boys chased other boys. Girls ran from them and shrieked. They looked in at windows and made little children scream. It was fun! "Whoopee!"

Then just for fun they surrounded an old man.

He tried to go on about his business, but they headed off every move he made.

"Leave me alone," he said. "A man should be able to walk down the street in peace."

The boys laughed. They were having fun.

But the old man didn't enjoy the joke. He was frightened. "Police! Police!" he shouted.

Before the boys could get off their stilts, a police officer appeared. The old man told his story. The boys tried to tell theirs. But all they could say was "It's Halloween! Doesn't he know it's Halloween?"

"It's lucky for you that it is," said Officer McBride sharply. "I want your names and addresses."

Now it was the boys' turn to be frightened. But they gave the officer their names and told him where they lived.

The officer looked very stern as he wrote the names and addresses in a little book. Then he

said, "I'll let you go this time because it's Halloween. But your fun is over. Get down off your stilts and go home. And walk! And tell your parents what I said, too."

The Wright boys couldn't tell them that night because their parents were asleep. And in the

144

morning they were gone. Only Katie was in the house and she was still asleep.

Then a neighbor arrived. While the boys were sleeping, she said, a policeman had come for their parents. Mrs. Wright had asked the neighbor to tell Wilbur and Orville.

"Policeman!" exclaimed both boys.

The neighbor went on, "There was a bad storm in the night. And just at dawn there was a regular cloudburst. The lowland along the creek was flooded."

"Why, there are houses there!" cried Wilbur. "We know people who live out there."

"Yes, and they had to leave in a hurry. Your mother and father are finding places for them to stay. That's why the policeman came for them— because your father is a preacher."

The boys looked at each other and grinned. Then they heard voices outside and hurried to the front door.

Mr. and Mrs. Wright had come and had brought a little old lady with them. She was Mrs. Annie White, and she lived alone in a cottage on the creek bank. The boys knew her well. She belonged to their father's church.

While their mother was getting breakfast, Mrs. White talked to the boys. She said it was lucky she was up and dressed when the storm struck. It had all happened suddenly.

"I heard an awful roar. I looked out and I saw a wall of water rushing down the creek. It was half as high as my house. I knew it would spread out as quickly as lightning. So I just left everything and ran."

"Didn't you stop to get your money?" asked Wilbur.

The old lady jumped from her chair. "Oh," she cried, "I forgot it! It's all I have in the world! It will be stolen!"

146

"You had it put away somewhere, didn't you?" asked Mr. Wright.

"Well, not exactly. It was in an old china teapot on my mantelshelf. I don't know what I'll do if someone takes it."

Mr. Wright was almost sure the police had placed guards to keep looters out of flooded houses. But he said he was going to the police station to tell about Mrs. White's money.

Presently Susan took the guest to her room. The boys were alone. They whispered together for a while. Then they went to the shed for their stilts. They had decided to get Mrs. White's money for her, before a looter got it.

Her cottage was a mile or so from the city. But they could go out there while their father went downtown. The water couldn't be very high now. Flash floods ran off quickly. Also there was a gravel road all the way. And a brick walk to the front door.

They were right about the water. It didn't begin to reach their foot rests. They splashed through it to the cottage door. And then inside to the mantel. There was a china teapot and the money was inside it. In fact it was full of bills.

Wilbur put them in his pocket and they left at once. They had reached the steps when they saw a man come from around the house. He wore rubber hip boots and carried a heavy cane. The boys thought he was a guard.

"Halt!" he ordered. "What are you doing here? What did you get in that house?"

Wilbur explained. The money was safe in his pocket now, he added.

"Are you expecting me to believe that story?"

"It's true!" exclaimed Orville.

"Give that money to me. I'll see the old lady gets it."

Something made Wilbur suspicious. The

man kept looking about as if he were afraid. A guard wouldn't act that way.

"Well, what are you waiting for?" the man asked sharply. He held out his hand for the money.

But Wilbur Wright wasn't that stupid. "Oh, no," he said. "I'll have to see your police badge first."

"Stop talking," said the man angrily. "Give me that cash and be quick about it."

Wilbur was sure now that this man was a looter. Mrs. White would never see her money again if he got it. Well, he wouldn't get it.

"I'm not waiting any longer!" the thief exclaimed. He lifted his heavy cane and started toward Wilbur.

"Help! Help!" shouted Orville.

Then several things happened all at once. The boys jumped off their stilts. Voices called from dry land. A gun was fired. Two policemen jumped from a spring wagon. Then they came splashing through the water in their rubber hip boots.

The looter tried to get away. Another bullet, fired over his head, stopped him. The policemen reached the cottage. One was Officer McBride.

"Well, if this isn't Slinker!" he said sharply. "We kind of thought we'd find you out here."

"I didn't take a thing, Officer. It's these boys. They took money from the house. They said they did."

Then Wilbur and Orville told their stories. And Wilbur offered to give the money to the officers.

"Take it to Annie White yourself," said Officer McBride. "I know all about it. Your father told us. Put Slinker in the back part of the wagon, Jim. We'll give him a free ride to jail. And I'll give you two boys all of the credit for catching him."

"I didn't catch him," said Orville.

"I didn't either," said Wilbur.

"You didn't run away, Orvy. You stayed right here to help if you could. And you had the courage to keep the money, Wilbur. I declare I'm proud of both of you."

The boys were pleased. They smiled at the officer as they fished their stilts from the water.

"Well, I guess I'd better fish you boys out of the water too. I'll take you back to town. Climb into the front seat but hold on to your stilts. Don't let Slinker borrow them."

"Would he try to use them?" asked Orville.

"He would, indeed. But not for walking. Come along now to the wagon."

The Boys Begin
To Invent

THE DAY Eddie Sines was thirteen he received a birthday letter from Orville Wright. Something in it pleased him very much. There was a big smile on his face. "Mother!" he cried. "The Wrights are coming back to Dayton! Orvy wrote me about it."

"Are they coming on a visit?"

"No, to live. Mr. Wright has been sent back to his old church. They'll be here soon."

"I wondered why Mr. Wright didn't rent his house in Dayton this year. He knew he'd be sent back. Now they will have a place to go."

"I wonder if Orvy still likes to take things

153

apart." Eddie smiled as he thought of that old sewing machine.

Within two weeks the Wright family were living in their old home on Hawthorne Street. Reuchlin and Lorin were with them, but only for a visit. They had work in Indiana now. In the fall they would enter an Indiana college.

After they left, Wilbur found full-time work in a machine shop. He was seventeen now and strong. He said the work wasn't too hard.

"He would do it anyway," Orville told Eddie. "He wants to invent things, and he thinks he ought to learn a lot about machinery first."

"Are you going to invent things, Orvy?"

Orville nodded. "Just as soon as I can think of something."

In the meantime, he was busy going to the old swimming hole again. And there were cherries and blackberries to pick.

Every now and then Eddie would ask Orvy if

he had thought of something to invent. At first Orville made excuses. He had been helping his mother. He had to fix Katie's doll bed, and so on.

After a time he began to worry. Why hadn't he thought of something? Maybe he never would. He was so worried he talked with his mother about it. "I can't think of a thing," he said. "I'm thirteen too. I ought to be making something."

"You can't make yourself invent," replied Susan gently. "You may get an idea from a story someone tells. Or from something someone does. Suddenly an idea will pop into your head."

"I wish it would hurry up and pop."

However, nothing happened until Mr. Starr came on Saturday. He had always brought butter and eggs from his farm on that day. But this time he brought butter only.

"Rats have been eating my eggs," he explained. "I didn't have any left to bring."

Orville began to have an idea.

"Why, they are eating up everything on my farm—corn, oats, barley, wheat. And now I'm missing my baby chicks."

"Don't you set a trap?" asked Mrs. Wright.

Orville's idea began to grow.

"I keep one baited day and night. I caught a few at first. But none now. They've become too smart."

"You ought to get a trap that doesn't look like a trap," said Orville. His idea had popped.

"That's a good idea, Orvy. I'd be willing to pay a good price for anything that would catch them."

"Maybe my brother and I can make one. We like to invent things."

"Go ahead. I'll pay you ten cents for every rat it catches. I hope you'll have it ready for me when I come next Saturday. I'm losing money every day."

That evening the two young inventors began to plan a new kind of rattrap. And it had to be something that would fool smart rats.

Orville had plans that Wilbur didn't like. Wilbur had plans that Orville didn't like. But at last they agreed and went to work. And by Friday it was finished.

It didn't look like anything ever set for rats. It was very large to begin with. It was really a little house with two rooms.

There was a front door and also a middle door between the rooms. The bait would be in the back room.

Just inside the front door there was a wide lever in the floor. When the rat stepped on this two things happened: The front door closed and the middle door opened.

Back of this middle door was another wide floor lever. The rat had to cross this to get to the

157

food. The minute he stepped on it, again two things happened. The middle door closed behind him and the front door opened.

Now another rat could go in. Then another and another as the two doors opened and closed. The boys thought the back room would hold five rats and maybe as many as ten.

Friday night it was tested in the woodshed. They didn't have cheese so they used salmon left from their supper. Both boys were sure they would catch something.

They did. A neighbor's kitten was in the back room fast asleep. The salmon was gone.

"Fish always draws cats," said Mrs. Wright. "Be sure to tell Mr. Starr about this."

Mr. Starr was surprised at the size of the new trap, but he was willing to try it. He said he would take good care his kittens weren't caught. He would use fat bacon for bait. Also he would keep a strict account of every rat caught. And

158

if the trap worked he hoped the boys would sell it to him.

The boys tried to decide on a fair price that evening. The trap hadn't cost them anything. They had used old lumber for the house and old springs for levers. The nails were old ones they had saved.

They finally agreed on one dollar. That would pay them well for their work.

Then came Saturday and Mr. Starr, smiling from ear to ear. "Boys!" he cried, "your trap has caught fifty rats! We got only one last night. I think we've cleaned them out for the time being. Here's your five dollars for the rats caught."

He gave the money to Wilbur and then said he'd like to buy the trap. "How much do you want for it?" he asked.

"A dollar would be all right," Wilbur replied. And Orville nodded.

The farmer shook his head. "No, that isn't

enough. Here are three dollars. And I'm glad to have it at that price."

The inventors were delighted. Eight dollars! They thanked Mr. Starr and said they would make another trap any time he needed one.

There was no argument about spending the eight dollars. Of course it would be used to buy material for another invention. The boys asked their mother to keep the money for them until they decided on something.

They talked about inventions every night in the family sitting room. Their mother listened while she knitted. Their father would have listened too, but he had to work on his sermons.

Sometimes Susan had to smile at some of Orville's suggestions. His ideas were popping fast now. Every night he had a new one.

There was his new kind of bootjack. One that would put the boots back on feet as well as pull them off.

Of course Wilbur had nipped that in the bud. He had said it couldn't be done. At least, they couldn't do it. A machine would have to be invented.

161

The next night Orville said he had thought of something they could make. "It's a washcloth worked by a lever in the floor. Press the lever with your foot and the cloth will begin to wash."

"How will it get behind your ears?" asked Wilbur.

"I didn't think of that."

"How would it go around your neck?"

"I guess you'd have to turn around."

"It's crazy! You'd have to be a tumbler to use it."

"It would work with a comb or brush, wouldn't it?"

"If you didn't watch you'd be combing your nose and brushing your ears."

The next day Orville said he had hit on something that was really good. "It's a long arm that will turn the pages while you read. You can use your hands to eat ice cream. Now then, what's the matter with that?"

"Everything. You wouldn't dare move. If you did the arm would hit your dish of ice cream. Then what?"

"I wasn't thinking about the ice cream."

"An inventor must think of everything. I failed with the flying toy because I didn't know enough about science. My science teacher had to tell me the secret."

"You mean, about the size and the power?"

"Yes. If you increase the size of an object you must increase the power that makes it move."

"You did. You put four fans on that bat you made larger."

Wilbur and Orville usually called the flying toy a *bat*. It had looked a little like one of those odd creatures that flew around after dark. And *bat* was easier to say than *helicopter*.

"Yes, but it was also much heavier. I should have used more fans and more and stronger rubber bands."

"Will you try that?"

"Of course. I'll never give up till I've made a bat that will fly."

"You've got bats in your belfry."

Wilbur laughed. "I know I have, but I won't try another until I know more about air and winds. I'd like to make some tests with a kite. I'd like to make one that would carry a load."

164

"I'd like that myself. I wish we could make one that could carry our coal and wood. Load it in the woodshed. Unload it at the kitchen door."

Wilbur nodded. "A kite big enough might do a lot of things—if the wind blew the right way. Are you willing to spend our money on one?"

Indeed, Orville was willing and he'd like to begin work at once.

THE MONSTER KITE CARRIED A PASSENGER

The boys argued for a week about the size. They finally agreed to make twin kites of oblong shape. They would fasten them together and so have one monster kite. It would surely carry a load.

But where would they make it? Their shed was too small. They would need a barn. They went about looking for one. At last they came across an empty barn a mile or so from town. The dwelling had burned down.

They lost no time finding the owner. They offered to rent the barn for one month. They explained what they wanted it for. Then they said they would move in at once if the rent wasn't too high.

"It won't cost you anything," said the gentleman. "You boys are trying to do something worth while. I want to help you. I wish you could make a kite that would do some of my farm work."

After thanking the gentleman, the boys went to buy their material—bamboo for the frames and cheesecloth to cover them, also a little varnish. The cloth had to be varnished to keep the wind from going through.

Only one of their friends knew about the kite. This was Eddie Sines. It didn't matter if he came to the barn. He was such a good friend that he was like one of the family.

The brothers began to make the great kite. Every inch of wood and cloth had to be measured. The same amount of varnish was used for each part, and the same number of small nails. Each kite must weigh exactly the same, even to the heavy rope tail.

The young inventors worked slowly and carefully. But at last the two kites were finished. And they certainly were twins. You couldn't tell one from the other.

Now they were fastened to bamboo poles. A space of two feet was left between them. One pole reached across the bottom from the outside edge of one frame to the outside edge of the other frame.

Another such pole was fastened across the top, all the way across both kites. A third pole ran across the center of both. These poles were to keep the kites from folding up in the wind. The heavy rope tails also helped to steady them.

The afternoon the great contraption was finished there was a good breeze. Wilbur, Orville and Eddie brought it from the barn. They held it up and ran along with it, waiting for the breeze to lift it. Then, of course, they would let go.

Wilbur held the string in one hand. His other hand supported the kite on the left. Eddie supported the kite on the right. Orville was holding the pole in the space between them with both hands.

Suddenly the wind blew harder. It was a regular gale. The kite shot up with such force the string was jerked out of Wilbur's hands. And Orville was carried up with the monster!

He hadn't had time to let go. Afterward he didn't care. Eddie and Wilbur were so frightened they were weak. What would happen? How long could Orvy hold on? Would the light pole break? Would the double kite dash him against something?

They thought of a dozen things in an instant. Then the wind changed and blew the contraption sideways into a tree. Of course Orville went with it. Now boy and kites were all tangled up together.

His arm was through one. Both legs were through the other. The tails were wrapped around his neck. The string was wound around his feet.

The other boys came running. They climbed the tree and cut the string. They unwound the tails quickly so he wouldn't choke. They tore the cheesecloth from his legs and arms. At last he was free.

Of course he could climb down, he said. He wasn't hurt. And he would like to have another ride like that, except the last part. It was wonderful to be flying through the air.

"It's too bad you couldn't guide it," said Wilbur. "There should be a way."

"What do you mean?" asked Edward. "Do you think a flying thing can be turned this way and that like a horse?"

"Why not?" asked Wilbur gravely.

"Why, because—well, no one ever did."

"Let's try it, Wilbur!" cried Orville. "I'd like to have another ride if I could pull the reins and keep away from the trees."

"I'd like to be a passenger, myself," said Wilbur.

Bicycle Pedals
and Gliders

"A new invention by Wilbur and Orville
Wright! A bicycle pedal that can't
come unscrewed! Ask at
Wright Cycle Co.!"

THIS advertisement was printed in the Dayton
newspapers one day in June, 1900. The next
morning the bicycle shop was crowded. The
owners, Mr. Wilbur and Mr. Orville Wright,
were kept busy explaining their new pedal.

"I don't care," said a young bicycle rider. "I'd
wait all day to buy their pedals for my wheel."

"So would I, Jimmie," said his friend Dick.

"You can't buy them here," said a man behind

them. "You can just find out where to send for them. The Wrights don't make them. They invented them and told a manufacturer about their idea."

"I wonder which one of the Wrights thought of it first?" Dick asked.

Jimmie shook his head.

The man behind them spoke again. "I don't believe they could answer that. They worked it out together."

"I'm glad they did," said a messenger boy. "It's dangerous to have your pedals work loose."

Other people said indeed it was and that every bicycle rider ought to be grateful to the inventors.

That evening two Dayton merchants were talking about the Wrights' pedal.

"Those young men could work up a big business," said Mr. Gerhart. "They could sell their pedal all over the United States."

"Yes, they could," agreed Mr. Blum, "But they won't. Their minds are set on something else. They want to make a machine that will carry a man through the air. They call it a glider."

"Oh! I've read about gliders. I can't understand how they get into the air in the first place."

"They say air currents will lift them and carry them along."

"Several men have been killed trying to glide. Don't the Wrights know that?"

"They do know, but it hasn't changed their minds. And it hasn't stopped their work on the one they are making."

"I didn't know they were actually at work on one."

"They have been for a long time. They use the room back of their bicycle shop."

"But their business!"

"Oh, they don't neglect that. The bicycle rush

is over by July. They have the fall and winter months for this other work."

"Well, it's a crazy idea and it won't work."

Before long everyone in Dayton had heard of the Wrights' glider. And almost everyone was laughing. Those Wright brothers were always doing queer things, they said.

For instance, Wilbur had been seen flying a large, queer-looking kite recently. It was during business hours, too.

And just yesterday Orville had bought a whole bolt of sateen. Of course he didn't need it. It was just a crazy idea.

In the meantime the "queer" Wrights were discussing the actions of the kite Wilbur had flown. It looked like two horizontal wings held together with light rods. A long cord was attached to each corner of each wing.

"Our ideas about balance were right," Wilbur reported. "I found I could control the kite easily with the four cords. I could keep the kite from tilting to one side or the other by moving the wing tips in opposite directions."

"That's just what we thought!" exclaimed Orville. "But what about dipping? Could you control that?"

"Yes, by moving the upper wing backward or forward. It worked every time."

"That's all we need to know," declared Orville. "That proves we can control a glider. We can finish it at once. I have the sateen."

AT KITTY HAWK

The inventors knew they couldn't glide near Dayton. They couldn't count on winds strong enough to lift a large glider. Also the winds there were not steady. This would make the glider bob up and down. They must find a place with strong, steady winds.

The United States Weather Bureau advised them to go to the coast of North Carolina. They could find such winds on a wide sandbar near the fishing village of Kitty Hawk.

By fall the glider with two horizontal wings was ready, and the Wrights went to Kitty Hawk. They were delighted with the place and made their camp near a high sand dune called Kill Devil Hill.

"It will be fine for take-offs," said Wilbur. "And there's not a single tree, Orvy!"

"And there's soft sand to fall on, Wilbur!"

They tested the glider first, holding it by long cords, such as they had used on the kite. It flew, just as the kite had flown.

Then came the great moment. They carried the glider to the top of the dune. Wilbur climbed on the lower wing and lay face-down. He grasped the bar that would move the wing tips. Orville began to loosen the ropes.

In spite of its load, the machine rose off the sand and up into the air, about eight feet. The brothers forgot their hours of hard work. The glider had lifted! Their ideas had been right, even if it did come down after a few seconds.

But improvements must be made. They must try out new ideas. They wanted to make an even larger glider. They had learned a great deal about air pressure.

This was just the beginning of many changes, new ideas and improvements. For several years the brothers went to Kitty Hawk every fall. Each time they tested a new glider.

Sometimes they were discouraged and ready to give up. Dayton people thought this would be a good idea.

"Why," said a mechanic, "that last glider of theirs did nose dives and stalled."

"If they don't quit now, I'll know they are crazy," said another mechanic.

"They won't quit," declared Edward Sines. "They can't. It's in their blood."

The brothers didn't quit. They thought of more improvements. They designed them and then made them. By the fall of 1902 there was another glider in the Wright camp at Kitty Hawk.

This one was a success. The brothers controlled it against strong winds. They were cau-

tious, however. They made no high flights. But they glided as far as 600 feet.

"Why don't you go up higher?" asked a guard from the government lifesaving station on the beach.

"Low flights are just as valuable to us," Orville explained. "We are learning to pilot our machine."

"We need experience," Wilbur added. "And we're getting it the safest way."

"Why do they want experience?" asked a guard that night at the station.

"They've got some plan they are working on," replied Guard Dough. "I wonder what it is."

"Well," declared Guard Etheridge, "they will never make one move until they know they are ready. They always think ahead."

"Yes," agreed Guard Daniels. "Did you ever know anyone to plan things out that way?"

"No, indeed, never," said the others.

A Great Day
in History

THE lifesaving station on the beach near Kitty Hawk was quiet one September day in 1903. Only two guards were inside, and they were reading.

Then Guard Dave Etheridge hurried in. "Boys!" he cried. "I've got news for you. The Wright Brothers have come back. And guess what they brought this time."

"Another glider," replied Guard John Daniels.

"Wrong! They've got a machine with a gasoline motor."

"A motor!" exclaimed the others.

"It's a power machine with a propeller."

"Didn't I tell you a year ago that they were working up to something?"

"You did, John. And didn't I say they would always think ahead?"

"You did, Dave."

"Well, they'll be out ahead of everyone in the world if this machine can really fly."

"Oh, I guess not," said Guard William Dough. "There's a Professor Langley who is making a heavier-than-air machine. It's supposed to fly soon."

"But it won't carry a load. This Wright machine can. It's the first flying machine ever made that can carry a man and fly under its own power. Mr. Wilbur Wright just told me."

"Is he going up in it?" asked Guard Daniels.

"He is and so is his brother. One at a time, of course. I hope there won't be a shipwreck that morning."

The others nodded and the guard went on: "And I wish them all the luck in the world."

"So do I. So do I," said the others.

However, the Wrights had nothing but bad luck for a long time. There were fierce storms and heavy rains. Gales almost blew their camp away.

They weren't ready to test the machine until the middle of December. By that time Professor Langley's machine had been tested. It had failed to fly.

The Wrights' first flight was to be on Thursday, the seventeenth. A track of wood covered with iron had been laid on the slope of Kill Devil Hill. Now the flying machine had to be dragged up the dune and put on the track.

But the brothers had plenty of help—five lifeguards. By Wednesday evening everything was ready. The whole village had been invited.

Thursday was cold and windy. Only two came

from the village: Mr. Brinkley and a boy of six-teen, Johnny Moore. Only three guards came. No more could be spared because of the stormy weather.

There were just five persons to witness a flight that would change the whole world.

WILL IT LIFT? WILL IT FLY?

"Well, Johnny," asked a guard, "do you think the machine will lift?"

"No, sir," replied Johnny. "I don't think it will. The wind is too strong."

"Those men certainly won't try to go up," said Mr. Brinkley anxiously.

The guards laughed. "You don't know them," said Mr. Etheridge. "They have already tossed a coin to see which one will go up first. Orville Wright won."

"Look! He's getting on it now!" cried the

boy excitedly. "Why do you suppose he's lying face down on the lower wing?"

"He can work the controls from that position," explained the guard.

"Wilbur Wright is looking at his watch," said Mr. Brinkley. "It's about time for the flight. It's almost ten-thirty."

"All right!" shouted Wilbur.

The engine roared. The spectators shouted. They were so excited they forgot the bitter cold.

The frail-looking machine seemed to shake in the strong wind that whistled around it. Could the plane fly? Would it be able to get so much as one foot off the ground?

The watchers had only a moment to wonder. Then Johnny gasped, "Look, look! It's moving. The machine is moving!"

Slowly and somewhat uncertainly, the plane was rising from the track. Then it rose higher as the watchers cheered wildly.

"It's six feet from the ground!" shouted Wilbur. "It's eight feet! Now it's ten! *It's flying!*"

The others yelled till they were hoarse. Wilbur was waving his cap and smiling happily.

After it had flown about a hundred feet, the machine began to bob up and down. Then it darted to the ground. Everyone ran to it. They feared the pilot had been hurt.

But Orville climbed out, smiling and happy. "How long was I up?" he asked Wilbur.

"Exactly twelve seconds."

"The front rudder isn't balanced just right. But it flew, Wilbur! It actually flew!"

"It's the first time a heavier-than-air machine has flown under its own power with a man aboard."

"Twelve seconds is only the beginning, Wilbur."

"It's only *our* beginning, Orville. Now we must work to make the airplane better."

In early September, 1908, Mr. Orville Wright flew for the United States Government. This flight was made at an army camp, Fort Myer, Virginia.

The parade ground was packed with officers and soldiers. They cheered when the pilot circled the ground.

"It takes a good pilot to do that," said a general.

"He is said to be one of the best in the world," said a major.

"Better than his brother?"

"Oh, no, they are both experts. They have been practicing for five years now, ever since 1903."

"I suppose the only way to learn to fly is just to fly."

Pilot Orville Wright gave the soldiers something else to talk about. He stayed aloft one hour that morning. And he flew for more than an hour that afternoon. Everyone was amazed.

That afternoon the officers met to arrange for the purchase of a Wright plane.

Great crowds watched Wilbur Wright fly in France in late September, 1908. He stayed aloft one hour and a half. In December he won a prize of four thousand dollars for a flight of two hours and twenty minutes.

The French people were thrilled. They begged just to touch the plane.

Princes, dukes and counts wanted to go up with Wilbur. But the pilot refused to be responsible for their lives. King Alfonso of Spain was intensely interested and had long talks with the inventor.

King Edward VII came from England to watch the flights. Many members of his court came with him. These English were just as eager to go up as the French. They were willing to

188

pay hundreds of dollars for one ride. But the pilot only shook his head and smiled.

Then came two travelers more welcome to Wilbur than all the kings in the world, Orville and Katherine Wright. They were just in time to hear the good news. The French government had decided to buy a Wright plane.

The inventors were now in Italy flying for the Italian government. Crowds watched at every flight. All were delighted with the soaring, white-winged bird. The King and Queen of Italy were daily visitors at the flying field.

The Mayor of Rome gave a dinner in his palace for the inventors and their sister. And then again they heard good news: Italy would buy a Wright airplane.

The Wrights were on their way home. They had been invited to stop in London. The brothers were received as conquering heroes there. Beautiful gold medals were presented to them.

In New York City there were more honors, more medals and banquets. In Washington President Taft pinned medals on the heroes of the air. As Katherine watched this ceremony in the White House, she wished her mother could have lived to see it.

Wilbur and Orville appreciated the many honors they received. But more than anything else, they wanted to go on with their work. They were sure that they could make the airplane better.

They went back to Dayton and started to work. Once again they used their small bicycle shop as their laboratory.

There was, however, to be at least one more celebration in their honor. This was given by the city of Dayton.

The celebration started on June 17, 1909, at nine o'clock in the morning. At that time all the factory whistles began to blow. Church bells

190

all over the city began to ring. For ten minutes nothing else could be heard.

There was a big parade, with many bands playing. Cannons boomed. Thousands of people lined the streets to cheer the famous brothers.

Wilbur and Orville rode in an open carriage. Ed Sines, Orville's friend since childhood, rode with them.

That night there was a huge display of fireworks. One part of the display had been made especially for this occasion. It showed the faces of Wilbur and Orville Wright.

The celebration went on the next day, but in a more dignified way. The Wright Brothers received medals from the Congress of the United States, the state of Ohio, and the city of Dayton.

After the celebration in Dayton, Wilbur and Orville went right on working in their little shop. They still were far more interested in their work than in receiving honors.

The Wright Brothers were not satisfied with their first airplane nor with any of the later ones that they built. As long as they lived, they worked to make airplanes better.

Today their first little airplane may be seen in the Smithsonian Institution in Washington, D.C. Only the best and most worth-while inventions are shown in this famous museum. The first airplane that Wilbur and Orville built belongs there, because it is one of the greatest inventions the world ever has known.